Secret of the Swans

Secret of the Swans

**A Novel
by Althea Hughes**

Secret of the Swans
Copyright (c)2019 Althea Hughes

Printed in the United States of America

ISBN: 978-1-54399-115-4

Althea Hughes
P. O. Box 114
Gakona, AK 99586
Alkenjack80@hotmail.com

Swan artwork by Randy Hughes
Cover design by Moontide Design
Production assistance from Book Baby
www.bookbaby.com

First Edition

This Alaskan story is dedicated to my Mother, Dora Byram Stadig (1903-2003), who fell in love with Alaska during her several trips here after my husband and I moved from Maine to Alaska in 1953.

Althea Hughes
2019

1

"There's the cabin!" Dad shouted over the roar of the plane as the bush pilot banked the aircraft and approached the ice-covered lake for a landing.

"That's the cabin?" I asked, struggling to make myself heard over the vibrations of the noisy engine. "It's so tiny—looks like it's growing right out of the ground."

"You'd better like it, Jeff. It's going to be your home for the next three months." I nodded and hung on to my seat as we settled down and taxied over to the shore.

A short time later, surrounded by piles of gear and supplies, my Dad and I stood on the shore of remote Tanada Lake and watched as the plane skittered across the frozen expanse, dipped its wings as it climbed, and then droned off into the deepening shadows of one of Alaska's highest mountains.

Dad pushed up the visor of his cap, put his hands on his hips and slowly turned all the way around without moving from where he stood. "Well, son, this is it," he finally said, "and it's just as beautiful as I remembered it was." His voice was quiet and hushed, sort of like how grownups talk when they visit a cemetery, real holy-like. I had the feeling that he would have said the same thing out loud even if I hadn't been there.

"Dig those mountains," I remarked, trying to rattle him out of his trance. "Makes our Oregon peaks look like ant hills. Does that big one over there have a name?"

Dad pulled his visor down into its original position and stepped closer to me. "Sure does. Tanada Peak— it's over 9,000 feet tall. And Mt. Sanford goes well over 16,000 feet." He pointed off to the right to the rough, sprawling mountain that looked like someone had taken a bite out of its side.

"Tanada looks higher, though," I remarked.

"That's because it's closer."

"Guess they like things big here in Alaska," I said.

"Speaking of big things, we have a big job ahead of us. It won't get dark until about 10 o'clock but it'll take us a while to get all this stuff up to the cabin."

"How far is it? Looked very close from the air."

"About half a mile. Sort of steep in spots but the trail levels off the closer you get to the cabin."

"I thought there would be more snow here since we had to come on skis instead of floats. The place is just about bare."

"The snow's usually gone this time in May but the ice won't be gone from the lake for another month—not until about the middle of June."

"I noticed open water at the end of the lake when we flew over," I said. "Glad we didn't have to land too close to it."

"It always starts melting there first," Dad explained. "A small stream dumps in at that end and helps to get the process started. The ice will get mushy pretty soon and nobody will be able to land with either skis or floats for a while. That's why we had to come when we did. But enough of the chit-chat, Jeff. Let's tackle the muskeg."

"What's muskeg?" I asked – but shouldn't have bothered because I found out soon enough. Dad's long legs seemed to work better than mine in avoiding the rounded clumps of dead grass which reminded me of my dog's head and sat like little islands along the shoreline. I kicked one of the tussocky mounds when we stopped to adjust our packs and told my Dad I wished my legs were as long as his.

"They will be someday," he assured me. I guess I believed him because folks were always saying how much I looked like the Nickerson family with my blue eyes, blond hair and skinny frame. And then after Mom had measured my height after my fifteenth birthday party, Sis started calling me lanky-hank.

The trail improved as we got away from the lake but the steep places and our heavy packs slowed us down. "It's a good thing we spent all winter jogging and getting in shape," I said. "Glad you kept me at it."

"Thought you might be," Dad replied. The trail finally took a sharp turn to the right and led to a clump of scrubby spruce trees we'd seen from the air.

Getting my first real good look at the old log cabin with its sod roof, I remarked, "Sure glad we didn't have room for the lawnmower or I'd have to mow the roof!"

Dad laughed. "Sod's good insulation and easy to get. Doesn't leak, either, if it's put on right. We might have to do a bit of patching, though. Worked on it some when I was here two years ago." I had a feeling of excitement as we stepped up to the cabin door and I could hardly wait for Dad to unwind the thong which held it shut. He pushed on the door but it wouldn't budge. A heave with his shoulder made it give way and it thudded awkwardly on one hinge. We soon forgot about the door, however. The small room was a kaleidoscope of half-opened cans, scattered tin dishes, feathers, pieces of torn sleeping bags and flour—lots of flour—everywhere.

"Phew! What's that awful stink?" I asked. "Smells worse than the time we hatched out the Japanese quail eggs in the living room!"

Dad didn't answer right away. After scanning the room, he finally let out a long breath that turned into a whistle and said one word: "Wolverine!"

"How can you tell?"

"That smell is a dead giveaway. When a wolverine raids a place, it usually squirts its stinky musk on what it doesn't eat—sort of like a calling card."

"But how did it get in? The door was closed."

"Look around and you'll find the place. They're great gnawers and diggers." It didn't take long. Back in the corner by the bunk beds was a place where something had chewed its way between the two bottom logs. I picked up a small bunch of dark brown fur and handed it to Dad.

"That's wolverine, all right."

"Think it's still around?"

"No, it's probably trimming someone's parka right now," Dad said. "Everyone likes wolverine fur even if they don't like their antics."

"Well, it must have had fun trimming this room. Worst mess I ever saw."

"Almost as bad as your room at home, huh?" Dad teased.

I wrinkled my nose and made a face at him. "Now, what do we do?"

"Not much choice. If you'll start swamping the place out, I'll pack the rest of our stuff up from the lake."

"What'll I do with the junk?"

"Pile it outside the door—we'll burn what we can and bury the rest. Don't want any varmints around. But let's get the fire going in the barrel stove first. These May evenings can get quite chilly once the sun goes down." Dad walked over to the funny-looking stove in the corner.

"I can see why they call it a barrel stove," I commented. "But I never saw an oil barrel with a door and a draft in the end, or with legs. Guess I never saw one tipped over on its side, either. And that flat piece fastened to the rounded top must be a good place to cook on, too."

"Right on, Jeff. You can buy a barrel stove kit in most of the hardware stores in Alaska. Guess some miner or trapper rigged this one up like this years ago. If you'll go out behind the cabin to the little lean-to and get some kindling and a few bigger pieces of wood, I'll see if I can straighten up that one goofy leg and check the draft." I was surprised to find a neatly stacked pile of wood, and loaded up as much as I thought I could carry. It was dry and didn't weigh as much as I thought it would. Dad looked pleased with my load. He went on to explain that it was a sort of unwritten rule that you never left an isolated cabin without a supply of wood, some matches and if possible, at least a little bit of food which wouldn't spoil in case someone needed it.

"Guess the wolverine knew all about the rule," I commented while I watched Dad stoke and light the fire. We both watched as little wisps of smoke crept up the rounded sides of the stove. But instead of heading up the chimney, the smoke started to billow out the heavy open door and into our faces. Dad shut the door with a bang, lowered the bar which held it shut, and motioned me to follow him outside the cabin. He pointed to the stovepipe sticking out a few feet from the rooftop—it had a large can placed upside down over the top!

"Want me to climb up and take it off?" I asked. Dad nodded and I shinnied up the staggered logs at the corner of the cabin. I had to twist and jiggle the container but finally got it off. Dad just kept on shaking his head as we headed back into the cabin.

"Thanks, buddy. First time I ever forgot to take the cap off the stovepipe before I lit the fire," Dad explained.

"What was the cap put on there for? Did the wolverine put it there?" I teased.

"No, it's just a good idea if you're leaving for a while to cover the pipe so snow or rain won't get in and rot out the bottom of the barrel stove. Promise you won't tell anybody in the neighborhood."

"Who's there to tell besides the wolverine? Is Bigfoot around?"

"No," Dad laughed. "But my prospector friend Sven will be stopping in one of these days, and then there's Joe."

"Who's Joe?"

"Joe Nilchik—we'll visit his fish-camp later on when we do the study plot down Tanada Creek. He has a boy about your age. His name is Jimmy."

"Neato! Wish he were here right now to help me clean up this mess."

"Guess we better get at it—or you'd better. How about if I go pack the rest of the stuff up from the lake now while you swamp a path inside the cabin? There's an old broom around here somewhere." Dad found it outside the cabin and passed it to me before heading down the trail with his empty pack. I had an uneasy feeling as he disappeared but knew this wasn't the time or place for a sissy and I tackled my assignment with vigor despite the broom's tendency to wibble-wobble. Wish I had the old vacuum cleaner Mom threw out before we left, I thought to myself—could have plugged it into a knot in one of those scrubby spruces!

By the time Dad got back with his first load, I had the bulk of the cabin's trash piled up in a heap outside. "Good job," Dad remarked as he put one arm around my shoulder and wiped his brow with the other. I could tell he was beginning to feel as tired as I was but everything needed to be brought up. "Can't leave anything for the bears," Dad said as he headed back for another load. I tidied up some more and then headed down the trail to meet him. He seemed glad to see me and gave me part of his load. "Guess you're already my right-hand man," he said.

"Hope so," I replied. "Remember you said I'd have to earn my keep." Dad grinned at me in a special way and we hiked on in silence. Stopping to rest a short time later, we both looked back at the mountains. Tanada Peak sat like a giant strawberry sundae as the sun eased its way behind Mt. Sanford, and a cool evening breeze reminded us that the long Alaskan day was winding down. And so were we. The cabin was a welcome sight and we swapped smiles as we entered into the warm and somewhat cleaner cabin than when we first arrived.

"Guess we have one more chore before we settle in for the night," Dad commented and walked over to the place where the wolverine had made its private entryway. "Don't need that extra ventilation so close to our sleeping quarters. We'll just duct tape some cardboard over the opening for now and put the repair job on our to-do list." I emptied one of the cardboard cartons and held it while Dad cut a fairly large piece and then covered the hole. As he finished, he held up the roll of tape and said, "Never be without this when you're out in the boonies! Now, how about some hot chocolate and some of your sister's cookies?"

I was all for it and ready to climb into the top bunk a short time later. Although I was tired, I lay there awake mulling over the events of the day. It all seemed unreal that we'd been in Portland in the morning saying good-bye to Mom and Sis and now here we were in the wilds of Alaska. I had a special cozy feeling about being in the wilderness alone with my Dad, and my thoughts soon became a blur of airplanes, wolverines, pancake flour, a smoking barrel stove and long legs sloshing through the muskeg. I thought I was dreaming when a loud, horn-like call punctuated the stillness and echoed around the head of the lake until muffled by shrubby tundra.

# 2

I woke up to the smell of bacon sizzling in a pan on the barrel stove and I could tell that Dad had been up for some time. Neatly stacked supplies lined the crude shelves above the slab table. Our jackets, caps, and anything else that would hang, decorated the corner space behind the stove. The sill of the one small window held a bunch of little things and the family picture Dad always carried. The whole cabin wasn't even as big as my bedroom at home but I guessed we'd be able to make out okay.

Crawling down from my bunk, I said, "Why didn't you call me, Dad? I'm your right-hand man, remember?"

"It's not really that late, Jeff. Feels like it ought to be noon but it's only eight o'clock. Of course, the sun's been up for hours and it looks like it's going to be a good day. I woke up early and decided to get some of our chores done so we could go exploring. How about some hot cakes and bacon?"

"Sounds good—smells good, too."

Before eating, Dad bowed his head and prayed: "Thank you, Lord, for the good night's rest. Thanks for the chance to be together in this beautiful country. Bless all that we do today and watch over Mom and Sis at home. Thank you for this food and that Jeff is with me. In Jesus' name, amen."

I gave Dad an admiring glance and dug in. "You

know, for a while I thought Mom wasn't going to let me come. She almost squeezed the bubble gum out of me at the airport. And Sis even looked sad when we left, but it was probably just 'cause she'd have to feed Tippy for the next three months."

Dad grinned. "Well, their loss is my gain. I've waited a long time for you to spend a summer here with me. Planned to bring you a couple of years ago but you came down with the measles just when I had to leave."

"How well I remember," I said.

"I was disappointed, too. It can get pretty lonely here. Anyway, this year's research should finish things up for me. Been coming here every other year since you were five years old. Your Mother's glad that the end's in sight."

"I know. She's always saying she'll be glad when you get through with the whole thing and get your doctorate—whatever that means."

"Well, it's a long story," Dad explained. "You know, I've been doing research on changes in tundra growth and its effect on caribou migration patterns and numbers. After this year's study I should have enough material to finish my thesis."

"What's that?"

"Just a fancy word for a report I have to do in order to get my doctoral degree. And speaking of a report, don't forget you have to do one to make up for getting out of school early."

I wrinkled my nose and said, "Did you have to spoil the day by mentioning that awful word 'school'?"

"Sorry, buddy, I won't mention it again—at least not until day after tomorrow!"

"Promise?"

"Promise. I won't even say 'school of fish' if we try for some grayling later on today. Should be a few of them in the creek by now."

"Yippee! Where's my fish pole?" I jumped up and knocked over the log stool I was sitting on.

"Easy there, son; got lots to do first. Besides the fish bite better in the evening."

"Well, let's get busy. I'm at your ..."

"Shh ...," Dad interrupted, cocking his head to one side. "Listen." He headed for the door and I followed him outside the cabin. Horn-like calls came from the direction of the lake.

"I remember now," I said. "That's what I heard last night after we went to bed. I thought I was dreaming."

"I hope they're what I think they are," Dad said. "Let's get the binoculars and go for a little walk."

We hurried beyond the spruces where we could see better. Two large white birds flapped their wings and paraded on the ice close to the open water at the head of the lake. Dad passed the binoculars to me and said, "Trumpeter Swans." His tone of voice told me that this was something special.

"Can we take a closer look?" I whispered.

"I think we should stay away from the lake today. They might be looking for a place to nest and we certainly don't want to discourage them. I haven't seen them actually nesting right here before. Sven had a pair of Trumpeters nesting in the pond over by his place one year—spent most of the summer watching out for them."

"They sure are big," I said. "Hey, they're swimming around in the water now. Doesn't seem like very much to swim in yet."

Dad nodded. "Hope there's enough to convince them to stay." We took our time hiking back to the cabin. Dad explained that the Trumpeters are the biggest swans in the world and were almost extinct at one time but their numbers grew and they were finally taken off the endangered species list in 1968.

"Statistics show that about four-fifths of these swans come to Alaska each year to nest. Hopefully a couple of them will like this place as much as I do," Dad added.

"I hope they do, too," I replied. "Why did they almost become extinct?"

"There used to be a big trade in swan skins. And there's a lot of eating on one of them—they weigh 25 to 30 pounds."

Reaching our cabin a short time later, we spent the rest of the morning doing some of the chores Dad lined up. Once in a while we'd hear the Trumpeters sounding off and we'd give each other the thumbs-up sign. Dad repaired the hinge on the cabin door, replaced the thong and installed a moose antler handle. He set me to work digging a cold storage hole in the permafrost.

"Have to dig halfway to China, won't I?" I sputtered.

"Not quite," Dad answered. "You'll hit frozen ground just a few inches down. I'll take turns digging, too. Have to make it big enough for the ice chest." He outlined the area with a rusty round-pointed shovel with a collapsible handle and then handed it to me. I was skeptical about the whole process.

"Have you done this before?" I asked.

"Every year I've been here."

"Why can't you use the same hole over again?"

"The old hole's sloughed in. We may even have to dig

another later on—especially if you keep us in fish."

"Well, if that's the case, guess I'd better get to work." Tangled roots hampered the digging but I plugged away at it, inching my way down into the frozen ground. The sun, now really high in the sky, beat down on me and I finally got so warm I took off my shirt. Strange country, I thought, shirt-sleeve weather but the ground's frozen solid. I was glad when Dad came to relieve me and then suggested we break for lunch. By mid-afternoon the cooler was in its special place and covered with spruce boughs for insulation. I was pleased when Dad said I had done a good job and that I was earning my keep.

"Got any energy left? Thought we might hike to the nearest study plot," Dad said. "Shouldn't take us too long to get there."

"How far is it?"

"About a mile. It's the closest one and it's pretty easy walking."

"Let's go." Dad gave me his binoculars to carry and he put a small pack on his back. We went around the cabin and headed up a gradual slope leading away in the opposite direction from the lake. We hadn't gone very far when Dad pointed up ahead.

"Looks like our Trumpeters are going the same direction we are." With long necks reaching out, they flew side by side, their huge wings making rasping sounds in counterpoint with an occasional trumpet call. They disappeared over the crest of the hill.

"Think they're moving out?" I asked, trying to hide my disappointment.

"I hope not—hard to tell." We tromped on in silence. The farther we got away from the cabin, the more countryside we could see. The scrubby growth got shorter and sparser as we approached a small fenced-in area almost to the top of the knoll. "We call this an enclosure," Dad explained. "I put four of these up when I first started my study so I could compare the browsed-over area with spaces the caribou couldn't get at. I've been collecting plant specimens, too, and making sketches over the years. Hope to someday publish a booklet on some of the rarer tundra plants."

"Looks like a bunch of dead weeds to me. Don't see anything green at all," I said, as Dad pulled a fat dog-eared notebook out of the plastic case he carried in his pack.

"It's still too early for this year's growth but these so-called weeds have their own story to tell." I detected a special excitement in his voice and I felt sort of left out when he got down on all fours and started to examine last year's tundra growth. Every once in a while he would look up something in his notebook.

Bored with waiting, I finally asked Dad if I could hike up to the outcropping of rocks not too far away. "Might find a specimen for my collection," I said.

"Go ahead. I'll be busy renewing a few acquaintances." I think I understood what he meant.

I'd been collecting rocks as far back as I could remember. I picked up a few volcanic-looking rocks and a couple pieces of shed caribou antlers; at least I thought they were caribou. They were lots skinnier than the moose antlers I'd seen at Grandpa Nickerson's. Sitting down on a mossy mound up by the outcropping and leaning against a big rock, I could see for miles around. Just like one big park, I thought, and then I remembered what Dad had told me about this area on our flight to Anchorage. Said over 13 million acres had been set aside back in 1980 as a park and preserve. It was named Wrangell something or other. Dad called it God's country and I could see why.

I sat sort of mesmerized as the afternoon sun wrapped around me like a blanket. I closed my eyes for a few minutes—or so I thought—and when I opened them Dad was standing by me and pointing down the slope and off to the left. "Caribou," he said quietly. "Lots of them. They're heading this way." He was right on. A large herd was playing follow the leader and clicking sounds punctuated the pounding on the tundra. An occasional grunt reminded me of the bullfrogs at Grandpa's pond.

"Must be over 200 in this group," Dad whispered.

"Are we supposed to be scared?" I asked.

"No, they probably won't even notice we're here."

Ranging in color from light tan to fairly dark brown and with some lighter hair on the undersides, tail and neck areas, the caribou were bigger than the deer I'd seen back at home. Some of them had antlers which weren't very big. Didn't look at all like the pictures I'd seen in an Outdoor Magazine article on a caribou hunt someone had been on in Alaska.

Although Dad had given me the quiet signal again, I couldn't help but poke him and point to a caribou directly in front of us. "How come the antlers are so small?" I whispered. "And the bigger animals don't even have any antlers."

"I'll explain later," Dad murmured. The main part of the herd kept coming and coming. I guess that Dad felt like I did—that we were witnessing an ancient ritual as much a part of Alaska as the beautiful scenery.

"Well, that was a special treat," Dad remarked as the last few caribou loped by. "I'd been hoping you'd get to see a migrating group while you were here but thought they might have already moved to their spring calving grounds."

"Where were you when you first saw them?" I asked.

"Almost here. I'd been keeping an eye on you and when I couldn't see you any more, I came looking. Didn't know you were asleep," Dad teased, "but I'm sure glad we could share this. When I first saw them, it seemed like the whole countryside was moving."

"What about the small antlers? Didn't look like pictures I've seen."

"This time of the year only the females have antlers and they keep them until shortly after their calves are born. The show-off males with those huge sets get rid of theirs after the fall mating season is over. And they grow new sets every year. Quite a system, huh?"

"Hey, Dad, look! There's another caribou running lickety-split. Must be trying to catch up to the others." Dad looked through his binoculars and let out a deep breath.

"There's a wolf chasing it, Jeff, and this is apt not to be very pretty." Dad put his arm around my shoulder and we watched as the large, gray animal caught up to the fleeing caribou and dragged it down. Ripping at the flank while the caribou floundered on the tundra, the wolf soon completed its kill and dragged it off in the opposite direction.

Pulling myself away from Dad, I clenched my fists and yelled, "I hate wolves!"

"It's undoubtedly a mother with pups to feed,"

Dad said almost apologetically, as if trying to justify the violence we had just witnessed.

"I don't care—I hate wolves!" I repeated and headed down the hill. I tried to hold back the tears but they spilled over just the same and I walked fast so Dad wouldn't see me cry. He kept several paces behind me all the way back to the cabin.

3

I didn't feel like eating much supper when we got back to the cabin but I could see that Dad was concerned about my attitude, and when he suggested that we go try to catch some grayling, I perked up and went looking for my fish pole. I tried to get my feelings under control but kept thinking about how that poor caribou had thrashed around before being dragged off. Then I tried to imagine what a bunch of wolf pups would look like if their mother arrived with fresh food. I wondered if they'd yip and squirm the way Tippy's puppies did when we fed them after she weaned them. And would they wag their tails? Surely was a puzzle.

I felt better as we approached a wide place in the creek below where we got our water. Dad showed me on a map how this stream flowed from the lake for several miles and then joined the Copper River on its long trip to Prince William Sound. The grayling would be heading upstream to their spawning area. I was beginning to wonder how in the world we'd ever fish without getting hung up on the alder and willow branches hanging out over the water. Finally, Dad led the way through the brush and toward a gravel bar in the middle. I could see now why he had insisted we wear our hip boots.

"Watch your step--these rocks can be slippery," Dad warned but I'd already found out when I slipped and got one arm wet. I was glad when we reached the gravel bar's firm footing. The water was calmer and deeper between the bar and the opposite shore and if a place ever looked fishy, this was it. Dad put his fly rod together and I fixed my spinning rod with a small red and white spinner Grandpa Nickerson gave me two years ago before he died.

"Stand down there near the end of the bar where the current starts to pick up again," Dad suggested. "It'll help keep your spinner from sinking and getting hung up. Let's see who can catch the first fish!"

"Righto!" And it turned out to be no contest at all because we each got a strike on the first cast.

"Keep your rod tip up and the line tight," Dad cautioned and it was good advice because the grayling didn't give up without a struggle. It wrapped the line around itself a couple times and I almost lost it. I took a good look at it after getting it in and untangling the line.

"Wow! This grayling's real pretty—has polka dots," I said as I stretched out the big fin on its dark purple spotted back. "Let's see yours, Dad." I walked over to take a look at his fish. "Aha, mine's bigger," I bragged. "How big can they get?"

"A twenty-incher would be a real big one. These are pretty good-sized. Yours must be at least fifteen inches; mine will go a foot if I stretch it a bit, just right for eating." It wasn't long before we'd each caught three more and I was really disappointed when Dad suggested that perhaps we had caught enough for the day.

"Gee whiz, can't we keep on fishing? This is fun." I just couldn't believe Dad meant what he said.

"This is all we need for now—have to eat fish all day tomorrow." Dad grinned as he knelt and started scaling his catch.

"Can't we get a few more and then just throw them back in? Grandpa Nickerson used to let me do that."

"No, but we'll come back here again when we've eaten these." I didn't say anything because I knew it wouldn't do any good. I took out my knife and started in on the fifteen-incher, which ended up being the biggest one of all. I had a hard time with the scales. I'd cleaned lots of brook trout before but nothing like this. Dad finished with his fish and came over and did two of mine. He had them strung on a willow stick before I finished cleaning my second one. "Nice string of fish," Dad said as he gave them one last swish in the water. We didn't say much on the way back to the cabin. I was still sort of put out because we had quit fishing so soon.

When we got back to where we could see the head of the lake, Dad all but shouted, "Guess what? They're back! Or at least I see one of them—no, there's the other one, too." The swans were in the water, and as we stood watching, one of them stretched its long neck and gave a loud call.

"Sounds like my French horn," I said, really cheered by the swans' return. "By the way, do they mind getting rained on?" Neither one of us had paid much attention to the clouds scurrying in from the south until sprinkles started making little ticking sounds on the bushes along the path.

"Looks like we might be in for a shower or two," Dad said as we hurried on to the cabin. "Shall we cook some of the fish tonight or wait for breakfast?"

"Let's wait for breakfast. Want me to take the fish out to the cooler on my way to the loo?"

"Good deal—sure nice having a helper."

Very willing to let this day come to a close, I climbed into my bunk and crawled into my sleeping bag. I felt I'd been on a roller coaster all day without being able to tell if I was up or down. Stretching my legs out as far as I could, I suddenly realized I wasn't alone. "Yikes!" I yelled. "There's something in my bed!" I hit the floor just in time to see a small, funny-nosed critter dash down at the end of the bunk and disappear.

"That's a shrew," Dad said when he quit laughing. "Better check your sleeping bag. It might have been a female looking for a place to have a litter."

"Oh, yeah, I'll bet." I thought he was kidding but decided to look anyway and didn't find anything except a bit of dried grass. "We've only been here a couple days and already the shrews are moving in," I commented.

"Well, you know what Grandma Nickerson used to say—a house wasn't a home until you'd seen a mouse inside. Perhaps this shrew was just the welcoming committee—trying to make us feel at home."

"It sure took my sleepiness away," I said. "And I'm wide awake now and I think I'm hungry. How about a snack?"

"Let's both have something to eat. How about a bowl of soup and some pilot bread?"

"Sounds good to me." I sat at the table and wondered how such a small animal could survive in this big country. As we ate, Dad explained that shrews really weren't rodents like mice were and that they ate mostly insects and spiders. They were loners for the most part except during breeding season which was anytime between March and August. So our visitor might well have been a female looking for a cozy place to have her young. I resolved then and there to always check the sleeping bag's innards before crawling in.

After we ate, I sat and watched Dad sort out papers from his study notebooks and put them back into his blue, waterproof case. Holding it up in front of him, he commented, "Doesn't seem possible that this little bundle represents over ten years of research. I have some of it already in the computer at home but have quite a bit more to go."

"What's that funny-looking tube sticking out the side of the case for?"

"This really is an inflatable bag. The tube is to put air into it if you wanted to cushion what's inside."

"Doesn't look like it's blown up at all."

"I don't put air in it often," Dad said, placing the bag back in its special place on the shelf. "Fits on the shelf better that way, too."

I climbed back into my bunk when Dad returned from a short trip outside, got undressed and reached to turn off the lantern which he lit while he was doing some reading. He suddenly stopped as if listening for something and pulled his pants back on. We both stayed quiet until Dad finally walked to the door and opened it just as a gruff voice called out, "Anybody home?"

"Well, come on in. What a sight for sore eyes! You look like a drowned rat!" Dripping wet and bedraggled, an old man eased himself through the doorway and didn't object when Dad reached up to help him get the pack off his back.

"I was hoping you'd be here. Didn't think I was gonna make it. Not feeling too good." Dad fixed him a place by the stove. The old man rubbed his hands together before he sat down. "Don't that fire feel good," he mumbled.

"I'll fix you some tea, and how about some hot soup?

Jeff and I had some a short time ago and there's some left over. I was wondering when we'd get to see you, Sven. By the way, that's my son, Jeff, over there on the top bunk. He just got chased out of bed by a shrew," Dad teased. "Jeff, this is Sven."

"I'm glad to meet you," I replied. "Dad has told me lots about you and how he likes to have you come visit him when he's here." We both watched as Sven took off his well-worn knit cap, letting long, unkempt gray hair out around his grizzled beard. He bent over and started to take off his wet shoepacs.

Stooping over, Dad said, "Here, let me help you with those."

"Nope, I can get them—don't reckon they smell very good." Dad handed him a pair of dry socks but the old man just sat and held them as if putting them on was going to take too much effort. He looked over at me and said, "Guess you'll have good company this year, Larry, with your son here." The words seemed to come from down deep inside his smelly boots and it was as if he had a hard time dragging them out. Dad handed him the soup and tea; sipping and slurping replaced the chatter.

"Good soup—tastes good. Heat feels good, too." He moved around on his seat and twisted his shoulders as if trying to get rid of his tattered jacket. Putting his hands on his knees, he leaned forward and tried to get up. Dad stepped over to him just as he lurched forward and started to fall, and then eased him over to the bottom bunk, helping him in and covering him up. Sven closed his eyes and low rumbles soon let us know he was asleep.

"Where are you going to sleep?" I whispered.

"Up there with you. Hope the shrew doesn't come back!"

4

"Don't wanna be putting ya out," Sven repeated over and over in the next several days as he struggled to regain his strength. He told what a hard winter he'd had and that he hadn't been able to get out for supplies. Joe Nilchik had stopped by and picked up a few furs he'd been able to trap and then later brought him in some stuff by snow machine. "He's been after me to get a snowmachine but I just figger I'm too old for that now. Good man, that Joe, good man. Gotta nice boy, too. Guess ya haven't had a chance to meet him yet, have ya?" Sven asked me.

"Not yet but Dad's been telling me about him."

Dad and I stayed pretty close to the cabin the first few days Sven was there. We scrounged firewood, patched the sod roof, did some work on the outhouse—but still left the front part open. We even built a tepee-like framework and covered it with plastic to use for a steam bath. Checking on the swans a couple times a day was the favorite chore as far as I was concerned. With the amount of water growing daily, lots of other waterfowl moved in on the lake, and evenings were a chorus of quacks, honks and trumpeting.

Sven seemed as excited about the swans as we were. One afternoon when he was feeling better, he and I walked down to the lake to get a closer look. We watched from behind a clump of bushes as the two graceful birds glided across the surface of the water as if propelled by a quiet, automatic machine which made them switch directions every so often.

"See that mound," Sven said. "They're buildin' their nest—build 'em out of bushes and twigs when they can't find an old muskrat house." The raised area was a short distance from shore and the swans had cleared away most of the weeds in the water around it. Often one of the swans would half-disappear into the water and come up with a mouthful. "Cleanin' up the place," Sven chuckled. "Guess we'd better git going." Getting going didn't seem very easy for Sven and after struggling to get up, he stayed hunched over a bit before heading up the trail. We rested often.

"Those swans really are a noisy pair," I commented during one of our rest stops. "They've been sounding off ever since we left the lake."

"Swans sing before they die; 'twer no bad thing did certain persons die before they sing," Sven said, and then hunched his shoulders as if half-embarrassed because he said it.

I was puzzled and when I asked Sven to repeat it, he seemed more embarrassed than ever. "Did you make that up?" I asked.

"No, some guy named Coleridge writ that. Found a book of English poems when I moved into my cabin years ago and I git it out and read once in a while. Always did like that one about the swans."

"I'd ought to learn it and recite it for my sister—she thinks she's going to be a big opera star someday. I usually have to plug my ears when she practices."

"You kin look at the book when you and yer Dad visit my place." And changing the subject, Sven asked, "Your

Dad showed ya any diamond willow yet?" I shook my head. Stepping off the trail a short distance, Sven took out the funny-looking knife he always carried—called it a bowie knife and cut off a piece of wood with odd shapes on the bark. "Ya can peel it and make a cane for your Grampie," he said as he handed me the piece.

"Don't have a grandpa any more. Grandpa Nickerson died two years ago just after Dad got back from Alaska."

"That's right. Your Dad was telling me. How about yer other Grampie?"

"Never had one."

"Oh," Sven said and we didn't talk much the rest of the way to the cabin. I spent the evening working on the willow stick and listening to Dad and Sven swap stories, Sven doing most of the talking. The bark peeled off easily on the smooth part of the willow and I liked the shiny white underneath. Sven warned me about peeling the bark off gently so as not to make any nicks in that part of the wood. He explained that the darker, diamond-shaped parts had to be whittled out. I followed his directions and I think it pleased him.

"Guess I'll make candleholders for Mom's collection," I remarked later, admiring the wood. "She likes wooden things."

"And what about something for your sister?" Dad asked.

"I already have something in mind for her. Gonna try to catch one of those shrews. Take it home and put it in her bed." Dad and Sven laughed, the wrinkles around Sven's eyes spiraling out and framing his bright blue eyes.

"That's my boy," Dad said.

"Nice boy," Sven murmured. His mood seemed to change and he was silent for a while. When he did speak, he said quietly, "I wish ..." but never finished the sentence.

I felt sad, too, at the mention of Mom and Sis, and I reached for the family picture Dad had put up on the window sill. I'd really never taken a good look at it before. We were standing in front of the fireplace. On the shelf above the fireplace were cedar boughs and some candles in Mom's favorite candleholders—two old hand-carved wooden swans which I knew Mom liked very much because she always had candles in them. I passed the picture to Sven and remarked, "Here's one for the rogue's gallery. Sis has that stuff around her eyes that makes her look like Dracula; yuck!"

"Now Jeff," Dad chided. "I notice you don't think she's so bad when she makes your favorite chocolate chip cookies. By the way, don't we still have a few of them left? Dig them out and we'll have a party. I'll make us some tea."

I got out the rest of the cookies and passed the box to Sven. He just sat there looking at the picture. "Have a cookie—they're delicious, even if Sis did make them." He shook his head and handed the picture back to me.

He didn't say much the rest of the evening and when we got up in the morning, he was gone.

5

"Think we ought to go looking for Sven?" I asked as we sat down for breakfast. "Why do you suppose he left without even saying goodbye?"

"That's our Sven. His moods are as unpredictable as the weather on Tanada Peak. He'll be okay."

"Well, he huffed and puffed all the way back from the lake," I said between bites. "You know, he quoted a line of poetry to me yesterday—something about a swan singing before it died but that some people ought to die before they sing. I thought it was pretty funny."

Dad laughed. "That's our Sven, again. I hadn't heard that one but often he comes out with something that really surprises me."

"Said I could borrow his book of poems. I really like Sven but I have this real funny feeling about him—as if there's a part of him hiding behind those squinty eyes and that beard."

"Well," Dad replied, "I think you're right. We've been real good friends ever since I met him that first year here but I don't even know his last name. He told me once that he came to this country from Minnesota in the early forties and that's about it. I respect his privacy and we always seem to have a good visit together." Dad shrugged his shoulders as if resigning himself to the fact that Sven was an unsolvable puzzle.

"He really likes the swans," I said, downing a second

cup of hot chocolate.

"I know. He's lived among the wild things so long that they're like family to him. He even made friends with a wolf once and didn't trap the area all one winter because he was afraid he'd catch it."

"Maybe he should've caught it—and all its brothers and sisters," I couldn't help but remark, remembering the caribou calf. "But why does he trap at all if he likes the animals so much?"

"Well, it's a matter of survival. It's a compromise he has to make in order to stay alive. He probably does what the old-time Natives used to do—apologize every time they killed an animal."

"By the way, did you check on the swans yet today?" I asked.

Dad shook his head. "I thought I heard them fly over when I first woke up this morning but then I got sort of distracted when I discovered Sven was gone."

"I'll take a look when I go after the water. Remember, the one who packs the water doesn't have to do the dishes—rule number two hundred twenty-six," I teased.

"Good try, old buddy. There won't be so many to wash now that our company's gone."

"I'm going to miss him. Won't have help eating grayling so I can keep on going fishing every day," I lamented.

"Speaking of fish, I thought we might head downstream tomorrow. One of my study plot's about halfway to Joe's fish camp. It's a good eight-mile hike. I need to spend about a day at the plot and then we could go visit Joe and see if Jimmy's there yet."

"Sounds good to me," I said. I picked up the buckets and headed for the creek. I scanned the whole lake area but couldn't see the swans anywhere.

"Sure hope they haven't left," I said when I got back with the water. "Looked like their nest was ready to move into when we were down by the lake yesterday."

"They might just be out for a morning spin," Dad suggested but not too convincingly. "And we'd better get spinning, too, if we're going to get everything done today."

Packing for a five-day trip was a bit more complicated than what I'd thought and when Dad helped me on with my load the next morning, I almost buckled under the weight at first. I felt better when I noticed him grimacing as he hitched his shoulders and adjusted his pack. We soon hit our stride, however, and the trail downstream was pretty good in most places. Every once in a while, Dad would suggest we stop for a rest, find a stump or a downed tree to sit on.

At one of the stops, we saw fresh tracks crossing the trail. "Caribou tracks," Dad explained. "More spread out than moose tracks, and not only that—the bottom of their hooves are curved in like an upturned cereal bowl. Great for swimming and their long migratory hikes."

"When did you learn all of this stuff?" I asked.

"That was many years ago. Your grandfather Nickerson and I came to Alaska one fall to hunt. That's when I fell in love with the country and promised myself I'd come back someday—but not to kill caribou."

"Think we might see some today?"

"Probably not—unless we get up in the open country away from the stream. Might see a bear though."

"Would you shoot it?"

"Only as a last resort. I've seen bears every year I've

been here. We respect each other but I usually take my rifle on longer trips where the trail's brushy. An old cow moose with a calf is not to be taken lightly either."

"I've been thinking about collecting some of the moose nuggets to take home to Sis. She could coat them with chocolate and feed them to her sissy boyfriend."

"Good idea," Dad laughed. "Do you remember the year I brought home moose nugget earrings for your mother?"

"How could I ever forget? I never saw Mom look so disappointed and disgusted in my life."

"Found them in a gift shop at the Anchorage airport. Got her some real gold nugget ones at the same time. She got all excited when I told her I had nugget earrings for her. I gave her the moose ones first. I'll admit, it was a corny joke. But," Dad paused here. "She forgave me—as she usually does."

"Miss her?"

Dad nodded. "You?"

"Uh, huh." We headed on down the trail.

After several hours of hiking, and despite frequent rest stops and a couple snacks, my back began to feel like it was on a hinge. I'd just about had enough for the day when Dad said, "We're almost there. Up that little knoll ahead and then down the other side." He seemed excited.

Knowing that we were almost there gave me a sudden burst of energy and we soon stood on top of the rise, ready to coast the rest of the way. Dad stopped suddenly. He pushed back his cap, let out a long breath and muttered, "What in the world?"

"What's the matter?" I asked.

"My study plot—it's all under water." Dad took off

his pack and motioned me to do likewise and I followed him down to where a small pond had swallowed up the trail, the trunks of surrounding trees—and the fence around the plot.

Dad pointed to the mound of sticks and dirt on the other side and said, "Beavers." Their dam was off to the left. "Looks like they dammed up the brook, built themselves a house and moved in. And they've done it all since summer before last. Guess I should've had my plot farther away from the brook. Never thought the beavers would move in."

"What are we going to do about it—break up the dam?"

Dad shook his head. "No, we won't break up the dam. We won't do anything about it. I'm disappointed. I did want one more season's data from this spot but guess I'll just have to get along without it."

I admired Dad for calmly accepting what he couldn't change—or what he felt he shouldn't change. I still thought he ought to make a hole in the dam and let the water drain out but he explained they'd only work harder to patch it up.

"Let's set up camp," Dad said and slowly led the way to where we'd left our stuff. I helped Dad with the small two-man tent and he fixed a fire pit while I gathered wood.

"Why do you suppose the beavers chose this spot to move into?" I asked as we sat down to our beans and pilot bread supper.

"Plenty of food handy. These poplars are scrubby but this is just about the only place they grow around here—right along that little brook."

"Why didn't they just cut the trees down, eat their dinner and call it quits?"

"Guess they wanted something more permanent. They have to build their houses in water deep enough so it won't freeze in the winter—and that's pretty deep in this country."

"Think we'll get to see them at all?"

"We'll go down by the pond when the sun's a bit lower. They're usually busy in the evenings. I'd like to take a good look at these thwarters of academia."

"What does thwarters of whatever you just said mean?"

"Just means they goofed up my research. Better dig out the bug dope." It was a good thing we did.

An evening chill settled over us as we huddled down on the shore of the little pond midst the incessant humming of mosquitoes and quacking of a pair of small black and white ducks down close to the dam on the other side.

"Buffleheads," Dad whispered.

"Think they'll nest here?"

Dad nodded, "They nest in trees." He put his finger to his mouth and pointed across the water to the beaver house. Leaving a wake behind it, a small brown head glided effortlessly along the surface of the water. Stopping now and then to give a big splat with its tail and then disappear, the beaver finally surfaced up at the head of the pond. He climbed out on the shore and groomed himself with his hind feet.

"Must be a female," I whispered. Dad grinned.

"The females stick pretty close to the house this time of year—the babies are just about due."

Tugging at a piece of wood, the beaver dragged it

into the water and headed towards the dam. "Spring repair," Dad said.

We sat trance-like and watched the beaver make trip after trip. Even the mosquitoes seemed a good part of the northland symphony and we let the evening's magic wash away the fatigue and disappointment of the day. Just before he got up and motioned that it was time to go, I heard Dad murmur, "Thank you, Lord."

6

Two days later, barking dogs and loud, rhythmic creaking let us know we were fast approaching Joe's fish camp. We'd followed Tanada Creek about eight miles beyond the beaver dam and I was just about done in when we began to hear river-talk and finally came to the muddy Copper. Joe Nilchik walked along the bank to meet us. He reached out his hand and said, "Larry Nickerson, thought you might be back. Been a long time—two years in July month. Miss you last year. You got son with you—looks like his daddy." He spoke in a quiet accented tone.

"This is Jeff," Dad said. "He's been a big help to me this year. Makes things easier for the old man. Where's Jimmy?"

"Have to stay in village to finish school. He's staying with Gramma. They come next week."

"How is your mother?" Dad asked.

"Doing pretty good. Had bad cold sick last month but better now. She like to come to fish camp," Joe said.

We walked down close to the shore where an odd-looking contraption ground out its raspy tune like an organ grinder. "Fishwheel," Dad explained. With chicken wire baskets and slanted chutes that aimed at a crude box between it and the shore, the fishwheel was anchored to two sturdy trees by heavy wires. The main part of the un-usual wheel sat on a raft of unpeeled spruce logs which sloshed around at the whims of the current.

"What a muddy river! Don't know why any fish would want to swim in it," I remarked.

"Fish like it—come back every year," Joe grinned. "Water's muddy all summer but clears up September month."

"How's fishing?" Dad asked.

"Not too many in yet—about twelve last night. Pretty good. Maggie's out back cutting fish." Looking at me, Joe continued, "Want to go see?" I nodded and we followed him past a white canvas tent set on a wooden platform. Maggie worked at a rough slab bench held up by tree stumps. Her long, straight black hair framed a pleasant face. She smiled shyly and nodded her head in greeting.

"Wow, Dad, take a look at those fish." I pointed to the plastic bucket of salmon under the bench. Maggie picked one up and skillfully sliced the meat off the bones, leaving a piece near the tail which joined the two sides. She made small cuts in the bright red flesh and then slung the whole thing over a rack made of peeled poles.

Maggie stopped her work on the salmon, wiped her hands on her flannel shirt and said in a soft, gentle voice, "I fix tea."

I asked if I could go pet the dogs. Joe told me that the one closest to the tent was friendly but not to go near the others. "What's the dog's name," I asked, pointing to the one he said I could pet.

"Yukon," Joe answered. "Lead dog for our team. I don't race no more but Jimmy won Junior Championship at Tok this year. Make me real proud."

Urged on by the wagging tail and the friendly look on the masked face, I approached the dog slowly and kept saying its name over and over. The pale blue eyes looked unusual on the dark dog whose fur was matted with pitch from the tree it was tied to. Must be shedding, I thought, noting the ratty-looking coat. The other dogs set up a howl, pulling at their chains and not quieting down until Joe yelled at them. Petting and talking to Yukon reminded me just how much I missed my dog at home and I sat there until Dad yelled for me to come see something.

The fishwheel had just dipped up a salmon and Joe said to keep watch because they often came in spurts. I reached the riverbank just in time to see the wheel scoop a wiggling fish out of the water and hurl it down the chute into the box.

"Way to go!" I yelled. "Oops, there's another one! Look at the size of that one, Dad."

"King salmon," Joe exclaimed. "First one this year!" He seemed excited.

"How'd you like to catch one like that, Jeff?" Dad asked.

"I'd sure like to try," I said, examining the giant gray-green fish with the reddish tinge.

Joe stepped down the bank to the box and picked up the fish after hitting it on the head with a stick. "Go about forty pounds, this one," he said and took it over to where Maggie had continued working on the fish. Dad and I followed.

"Ah, big one," she said, beaming broadly. "Lotsa work." We watched as she skillfully cut down the middle of the big salmon and took the insides out. Big bunches of reddish-orange eggs slithered out with the innards.

"Sure would like to have a bunch of those eggs," Dad said. I looked at him as if he'd lost his marbles. "Need something fresh for breakfast," he continued, winking at Joe.

"Take all you want," Joe said. Dad went to get a small container from his pack. I decided to go sit by the fishwheel and wait for more action. Dad and Joe came and sat chatting nearby and I half listened as they talked about caribou, beavers, trapping and problems in the villages. At one point I heard Joe say: "Hard to know what to do. Old people dying off and young people don't follow the old ways no more. Sometimes I have a hard time telling Jimmy how I feel. Seems like we're losing our kids."

"Lots of folks are having trouble with their kids nowadays," Dad said. "I think they have harder decisions to make than we did when we were young. Takes a lot of wisdom from the Lord to bring them up right." Joe nodded.

I felt drowsiness settling in and decided I'd better get up and move around some before I embarrassed myself by going to sleep. I walked back to watch Maggie again for a while. She looked at me and smiled. "My boy Jimmy be glad to meet you," she said softly.

"I'm looking forward to meeting him, too," I answered. I liked this friendly woman and her quiet manner. When she went to dump a bucket of fish scraps into the Copper, I walked along with her and decided to explore the path leading downriver.

A short distance down the trail was a small structure with a pile of dry wood stacked outside the entrance. Must be the smokehouse, I thought, although it obviously wasn't being used. When I walked past the building, I noticed a large white skin of some sort stretched out on the far wall. Stepping up to get a closer look, I was amazed to see that it had feathers all over it. I reached out and touched the bottom of the skin—it was damp and somewhat bloody. "Oh no," I said out loud as the reality of my discovery set in, "not our swan." I hurried back to where Dad and Joe were standing. Dad was putting the bag of eggs into his pack.

"Thanks a lot, Joe," he said. "We'll have to get the boys together when Jimmy gets here. Thanks for the tea, Maggie. Be sure to stop to see us if you're up our way. The welcome mat..."

"Dad," I interrupted, "I saw ..." I didn't finish because he gave me one of his 'don't you dare say a word' looks, put his hand firmly on my shoulder and pointed me in the direction of the trail.

"We're going, Jeff," he said. "Say goodbye." I lifted my arm and mouthed the words halfheartedly. After we'd gone a short distance Dad stopped, looked back and waved at Joe and Maggie, still standing where we'd left them. They waved back.

I waited until we were quite a ways from the camp before I started in. "Dad, I saw a white skin with feathers on it stretched out on the smokehouse. I just know it's our swan. That's what I wanted to tell you."

"I had a hunch that was what you wanted to talk about," Dad said. He hesitated for a moment as if struggling for the right words. "Yes, it's a swan skin—and it may be our swan. Joe told me he found it dead upstream two days ago."

"Well, I don't believe it," I blurted out. "He probably just told you that so you wouldn't turn him in. I think he's lying."

"Don't talk like that," Dad scolded. "Joe said it was

dead when he found it and that's that."

"Well I don't care if I ever go back there again. I suppose he'll be out trying to get the beavers, too, now that he knows they're there." I skirted one side of a muddy area and Dad went on the other.

When we came together again, Dad said quietly, "He already did."

7

"This stuff sure is stinky—messy, too," I said as I tied little clumps of the salmon eggs inside small, red mesh squares Dad had pulled out of his pack.

"Well, those eggs were fresh yesterday. If you think they're smelly now, just wait a few days," Dad replied.

"For a while I really thought you were going to make us eat them."

"Some folks think they're a great delicacy and pay big money for them—guess we'll just use them for bait. Say, you're doing a good job there, buddy. That ought to be just about enough." Dad had already rigged the pole with 40-pound test line and a pencil lead sinker tied on about two feet from the huge hook. He baited the hook with one of the mesh bags of salmon eggs.

"This pool almost looks like our grayling hole with the gravel bar in the middle," I said.

"Lots deeper," Dad commented. "Current's swifter, too, especially below that big rock. The quieter water above the rock makes a good resting place. They may not be in here yet, but we'll give it a try." He handed me the outfit.

"Wow, I've never fished with such a heavy pole. That sinker makes it feel like there's fish on already."

"I know," Dad said. "Takes a while to get used to the feel of it. Cast downstream into the current and let it sink until you feel it bobbing on the bottom. Then reel it up slowly until it gets on this side of the rock."

The first try was a bummer as the line caught in some scraggly bushes struggling for survival on the gravel island. The second cast found the hook, line and sinker in a heap at my feet. "Third time never fails," Dad said, and his prediction was right. I kept jerking on the pole as the sinker played games with me and made me think I had a fish on but I soon got the hang of it. It was hard work, though—casting and reeling, casting and reeling.

Finally passing the pole to Dad, I said, "Here, you try it for a while. My arm's beginning to feel like a grizzly's been chewing on it."

"Guess I'll put on new bait. This one's sort of raggle-taggle," Dad said, noticing the faded eggs and ripped mesh. I sat on a rock and watched the rhythm of Dad's casts and how he paced his reeling in, always keeping his rod tip high. Must be hung up, I thought, when at one point the tip of the pole arched and Dad leaned back and braced the handle firmly on his stomach. I looked down the length of the line just as a huge fish lunged out of the water, did a flip-flop and then disappeared in a swirl of foam and splashing.

"Here, take the pole and hang on tight!" Dad yelled.

"No, it's your fish!"

"Don't argue—take the pole!" I followed his orders.

"Feels like a whale—don't know if I can hang on!"

"Brace the pole against your belly. Hold tight with your right hand and reel with your left. Here, let me loosen the drag a bit." The line zinged as the fish headed downstream and beyond the big rock. "We're going to have to follow it!" Dad yelled. "Come on!" He helped me along so I wouldn't lose my footing. Once in a while I'd feel a bit of slack and reel in, afraid that I'd lost it. The big fish led us a royal chase.

"Guess he's headed back to the Copper," Dad said. "Hang in there—we'll go along with him. Keep the line tight! Looks like he might be tiring a bit." After what seemed like a lifetime, the fish eased itself into a shallow pool near the shore. It gave one final leap, splashing us both, and I started to lift the pole.

"Don't lift the pole!" Dad warned. "You'll break the line. Just keep working it gently toward shore. Atta boy, little bit more—got it!" He reached in and pulled the fish out of the water.

"Whew! It almost got me," I said. We stood back and admired the catch.

"Well, son, I'm proud of you—your first king salmon. Fishing will never be the same for you again, that is until you catch another king!"

"But, Dad, that was your fish—you hooked it."

He reached over and gave my cap a little twist. "How about if we call it a joint venture?" I nodded.

"How much do you think it'll weigh?" I asked.

"Probably about 35 pounds—don't think it's quite as big as the one we saw at fish camp."

"Don't mention fish camp," I sputtered.

"Wouldn't have caught the fish without those salmon eggs," Dad reminded me and he set about cleaning the fish. "Guess I'll just fillet it out so we won't have so much to tote. Besides I think those gulls should be rewarded for their patience." Eyeing our catch, several of the birds swooped over the creek and squawked for scraps. Dad further explained, "The smaller ones are Mew Gulls and the bigger ones are Herring Gulls. Measured from the end of the beak to the tail, Mew Gulls are seventeen inches long and the Herring Gulls stretch out to twenty-four inches."

"Can the Mew Gulls purr like a cat?" I asked. Dad raised his eyes, winked and shook his head. "Guess the Herring Gulls must like fish," I said.

"You got it, buddy."

"Looks like you've done this before," I commented as Dad sharpened his knife and went about skillfully filleting the fish. He made a cut behind the head to the backbone and then angled his knife and sliced back to the tail where he cut through, ending up with a long strip of bright red meat. The next cut removed the backbone and tail from the other side. The head came off next and was soon being air-freighted by an eager gull.

"Fresh salmon for supper," Dad said, rearranging our packs so that he had most of the bulky stuff. "You can carry your fish and my blue research bag." Blowing some air into the bag, he explained that it would be softer in the pack.

"Think we'll make it home by suppertime?" I asked.

"Not unless we dine fancy and eat late. We've still got several miles to go. We're not too far from the beaver dam—we'll stop in for lunch. We could try for home today—it'll be daylight until the wee hours."

"I'm game if you are. If I play out you can drop me off at a fish hole and come back for me in a week or two, that is if you still want me around."

"You haven't exactly been Uncle Cheerful the last day or so but I guess we're all allowed an off day now and then."

"Thanks, Dad," I said, "when is yours?"

"I'm just storing them up," he said, shouldering his pack. "Beavers, here we come!"

There was evidence that the beavers had been busy the few days we'd been gone. They'd widened the dam and cut down several trees on the upper end. We joined them for lunch and noticed that they weren't the only busy critters around.

"Hey look, Dad, did you see that? A duck just flew out of a hole in that tree."

"That's probably one of the buffleheads we saw here before. Remember, I told you they nest in trees. Guess that pair decided to stay. Good deal."

"Ever see one nesting before?"

"No, never did. That hole's pretty high up, isn't it?"

"Must be a sight when they push the little ones out of the nest—guess mama gives them a shove and yells 'bombs away!' Sure would be fun to see them."

"Well, maybe we will. But right now we'd better keep our eyes on the weather. Looks like one of those quick summer showers moving in—probably already raining cats and dogs at home. That creek can come up pretty fast, too." But the weather was the least of our worries a short time later when we headed up a short incline. Dad's long legs outpaced mine as usual, and when he stopped abruptly, I thought it was to let me catch up. Then I noticed he was backing slowly towards me. Pointing slightly to the right, Dad whispered, "Bear up ahead."

Tagged by a small, black fluff of fur, a large brown bear stepped into the trail. "Grizzly?" I asked, feeling a funny sensation on the back of my neck.

"No, it's a brown phase of the black bear—mother with cub." Not having good eyesight but sensing the presence of danger, the she-bear kept on coming slowly towards us. Stopping every now and then, she sniffed the air and at one point stood up on her hind legs. Getting down on all fours again, she cuffed at the cub following her as if trying to tell it to stay out of the way. And we made haste at getting out of the way, too, because she came barreling down the path. Puzzled, however, when she stopped abruptly, we soon saw the reason when a little brown cub crawled out of the bushes.

"Well, I'll be darned," Dad said as we watched from a distance. "She had two cubs. No wonder she got so excited. We walked past that little bugger without even seeing it. And it looks like we won't be taking that trail home. We'll have to go back and try the trail nearer the creek."

The rain had moved in and was turning out to be more than a summer shower. The trail sloshed up fast and slowed us down considerably, but when we came to a gully near a swampy area, it didn't look much worse than what we'd just come through.

"Guess we can make it okay," Dad said and I followed him across the gully and into the taller brush which grew canopy-like over the trail in spots. I did my best to keep up to him but the mud got deeper and the brush kept reaching out and grabbing my pack. Dad kept looking back to make sure I was coming.

Finally, I was encouraged by an open space up ahead—like the end of a tunnel. The elated feeling didn't last long, however. Dad stopped and the worried look on his face warned me that something was wrong.

"The water's come up higher than I thought it would—too deep to wade," he said. The water had overflowed the stream and cut a channel right across the trail.

"Now what do we do?" I asked.

"We'll hightail it back and hope we can get across where it runs back into the creek. I've seen it do this before but have never been caught in it. It makes a little island here until the water goes down again."

"I think I'd rather swim across than go back the way we came."

"Sorry, buddy, back we go—and on the double!" Charging through the mud and brush, we finally came to the gully we'd so easily crossed a short time before. It was fast filling with water.

Looking the situation over, Dad said, "You wait here. I'll take my pack over and then come back for you. It's been a long time since I gave you a piggyback ride."

And it's going to be a lot longer, I said to myself, and plunged into the rising water behind him. It was deeper than I thought. Dad crawled up the other side, took his pack off and turned around to see me floundering in the muddy water. He dove into the channel and reached me just as my pack rose to the top of the water and floated itself loose.

"Grab the pack!" I yelled, but Dad grabbed my arm instead and guided me across the swirling water. The swift current carried the still-floating pack down into the creek, around a bend and out of sight.

8

I couldn't ever remember being so miserable in my life and being soaked to the skin was the least of my misery. When Dad said he was going downstream to look for the lost packsack, it suddenly dawned on me why: the blue research case was in it. I began to shiver and the chill which ran through my being had a good measure of fear mixed in. "Why hadn't I followed Dad's directions?" I kept asking myself over and over. The roar of the rampaging creek, the howl of the wind and the pelting rain all seemed to be chanting out why, why, why?

Despite my grief over the turn of events, I realized that I had to somehow get a fire going and try to dry my wet clothes. I took the ground-cloth out of Dad's pack and draped it over some branches so that it made a tent-like shelter. Finding the waterproof case with the matches was easy compared with the chore of finding some wood that would burn. Everything on the ground was soggy so I looked for dead branches on the undersides of the willow and alders. I gathered several bundles and put them inside the shelter while I scuffed out a crude fire pit nearby. After whittling through the wet wood to the dry inner part and making a little pile of shavings, I used several matches before a tiny flame curled around the kindling enough to make it crackle. I soon had a good fire going and more wood piled.

Taking off my rain jacket, I turned it wrong side out

and hung it under the "roof" but near enough to the opening to get some heat from the fire. I took my boots off and dug out the extra pair of socks from Dad's pack, along with some waterproof bags which I put on over them. Huddling under the makeshift shelter, I couldn't help thinking about Dad and how disappointed he must be with me, besides being as wet and cold as I was. I kept listening for the sound of his footsteps but it was hard to hear anything over the roar of the water. The wind died down somewhat and the rain tapered off, but fog moved in and shrouded everything in its murkiness. I had never felt so alone in my life.

I kept looking off to the right in the direction Dad had gone, so I didn't see him approaching from behind the shelter. Hearing strange noises, I sat perfectly still and a tingling sensation running up and down the back of my wet neck brought on the shivers. A sense of relief washed over me when Dad's familiar voice called out, "Hey, Jeff, I'm back!"

Jumping up, I ran to meet him and when I saw the wet packsack slung over his shoulder, I yelled, "Eureka, you found it!" Dad didn't say anything but stood there surveying the scene.

Drawing me to him, he squeezed my shoulders and said, "You're quite a woodsman. Looks like you've got things pretty well under control. Boy, am I wet! Had to jump in again to get this. It caught up on a snag close to the shore but I still had to go into the water." When he put the pack down on the ground, I noticed how limp it was.

"Where's the stuff that was in it?" I asked, fearing the worst.

Dad hesitated, looked down at his feet, and then said quietly, "It was empty."

"Empty?" I whispered, hoping I'd heard wrong. Dad nodded his head and set about digging in his pack for something to eat. I walked over and stared into the gully, now a busy slough hustling on its way to the creek with its load of debris picked up along the way. I had a sad, empty feeling as if nothing mattered any more. The only other time I could remember feeling like this was when Grandpa Nickerson died and I'd wanted to go off by myself where I could struggle with the tight band which kept winding itself around my chest. I started to cry and the next thing I knew Dad was leading me back to the shelter.

"Let's have a bite," he said, "and I think we'd better say thanks before we eat." I bowed my head and listened while Dad prayed: "Thank you, Lord, for your protection today. Thank you for the chance to catch the big fish. Thank you that Jeff is here with me. Bless this food and go with us the rest of the way home. In Jesus name, amen."

"How can you be thankful that I was with you today?" I blurted out between sobs. "I ruined everything!" If only Dad had jumped up and down and yelled at me or called me a disobedient brat—or even cut a switch and used it—that would have been easier to take. But to say he was thankful I was with him—I buried my face in my knees.

Putting his hand on my shoulder, Dad spoke softly, "I'm not happy about what happened today but it could have been worse. I'm partly to blame because taking the trail through the swamp wasn't a very smart thing to do."

"But if I'd done what you told me, I wouldn't have lost your stuff."

"That's right, Jeff, and what you did was wrong. We can't change what happened but we can change how we face up to it. You're still my son and I know you're sorry so that makes two of us. Let's eat—it's a long way home."

9

"Guess what, Dad? There's a swan sitting on the nest down at the lake!"

"Good deal—must be the female. I was hoping she'd keep on with her project. And now maybe you can get yours started. I've got mine cut out for me," Dad said and I knew exactly what he meant.

"Dad, did losing your stuff mean your whole study is shot and you'll have to start over again?"

He hesitated before answering. "No, it's not completely down the drain. I have a lot of the statistical information in the computer at home, but all my original notes and of course the sketches for my book were all in the bag. I may have to come back here another season if I want to carry through on the book project."

"Guess you won't bring me back here with you again." I said, "and I wouldn't blame you a bit. Maybe you'd be better off bringing Sis—even if you'd have to charter an extra plane for her makeup!"

"Be fun to have the whole family here, wouldn't it?"

"Be nice to have Mom doing the cooking."

"Getting tired of mine?" Dad asked.

"Getting tired of those dried eggs."

"How about getting us a feed of grayling for supper?"

"You mean it—can I go by myself?"

Dad nodded. "You're the fish provider from now

on—I'm going to be too busy." And his words were right on.

The days settled into a fairly regular routine with Dad making several trips to the two study plots nearest the cabin. He collected specimens and sat up late at night making sketches. I kept tabs on the nesting swan, packed the water and wood, did the dishes—and best of all, kept us in fresh grayling.

As I approached the grayling hole one day I could see that something was different. The pool was boiling with newcomers—the sockeyes had moved in. Darting here and there and doing an occasional flip-flop out of the water, they made an ever-changing pattern in the clear stream. When Dad came to take a look, he suggested that I not fish here for a while. Sensing my disappointment, he said, "You can come watch them, though. Just keep your eyes peeled for bears. They do love fresh fish."

Watching the salmon became a favorite activity each day—despite the bear warning. The long, warm sunny days had helped to lower the water level in the creek and a grassy island hummock appeared a short distance from shore above the pool. Thinking that would be a good salmon-watching spot, one day I took off my boots and waded out to it. I balanced myself on the highest part and let my feet dangle in the water, combing the long, slim grass with my toes. It felt good. When they started to get chilly, I pulled them out of the water and hunched over, hugging my knees.

Closing my eyes, I concentrated on the sounds around me: the boisterous cries of the gulls, the gentle stream chatter, and the continual whomps of the spawning salmon. I felt as if I was the only person in the world and began to sway gently as if caught up in a rhythm of life that I couldn't control but that left me with a feeling of peace. I didn't hear the approaching footsteps or see the quiet figure that appeared on the edge of the stream.

A splash from a stone close to my island jarred my dreaming and I looked over to see Joe Nilchik standing on the bank, smiling, and with the butt of his rifle resting on the toe of his boot. "Sorry to bother you," he said, "but thought you might go sleep and fall in."

Eyeing the gun and the pack on his back, I blurted out, "And it would be none of your business even if I did!"

Joe looked down at his feet and seemed puzzled by my rude reply. Turning to leave, he asked, "Where's your daddy?" I pointed in the direction of the cabin. Joe disappeared up the path away from the creek.

I splashed my way to shore, dressed my feet and tried to decide what to do. My mind was in a turmoil—how could such a beautiful day turn sour so fast. Why did Joe have to show up and spoil it? He was probably going after the other swan. The least I could do was try to stop him. I wondered what Dad's reaction was going to be when Joe told him about my smart-aleck remark.

After dragging my feet all the way back to the cabin, I stopped outside to try to muster up enough courage to go in and face the music. The loud talking and laughing coming from inside the cabin made me curious and I went in. Noticing Dad's happy look and Joe's broad grin, I looked from one to the other. "Good news, Jeff," Dad said with an unusual huskiness in his voice. "Look!" He held out the lost blue research case. "And it's all here. Joe found it and hiked all those miles to bring it to me."

My mouth popped open and I stepped over to Dad and reached out and touched the precious bag. I wasn't dreaming—it was there—all of it, and the sorrow and worry of the past week peeled off and left me light-headed. I couldn't think of a thing to say. But what should have been one of the happiest moments of my life had a dark cloud hovering over it, a dark cloud made up of feelings for shame and embarrassment over my rudeness to Joe. I knew I had to do something about it but there never did seem to be a proper moment.

Joe stayed for lunch but got ready to leave shortly after. "Maggie's by herself," he explained. "Jimmy and Grandma coming soon. My brother Fred send me Caribou Clatter—he plans to bring them in with the swamp buggy. Too far for my mother to walk no more."

Dad shook his hand over and over again as he prepared to leave and said, "Don't know how I can ever thank you. You're a real friend."

Joe smiled and said, "See you," and disappeared down the trail.

Dad bustled about, cleared off the table and soon had it covered with notebooks and papers. He kept shaking his head and grinning as if he couldn't believe his good fortune. Joe had found the bag about two miles upstream on the creek when he was out hunting rabbits. It had hung up on a small island in the middle. Recognizing the familiar blue case, he'd waded out and retrieved it.

"Did any of the stuff get wet?" I asked.

"No, just beat up a bit but not too bad. Putting that air in helped a lot. We can be thankful for that." Dad didn't seem to notice that I wasn't sharing his enthusiasm, so caught up was he in the turn of events. I spent the rest of the afternoon outside, miserable every minute. I knew I'd done wrong—again—and that something would have to be done about it. That chance came at suppertime.

"This has been such a great day—let's both give thanks," Dad said. Not knowing how to get out of it, I nodded my head. Dad prayed first.

I followed with words that seemed to pop out all by themselves—especially the last part when I prayed, "And forgive me for being rude to Joe, amen." I opened my eyes but kept staring into my tin plate. Picking up my fork, I moved my food from one side to the other. A great quietness had seeped into the room and even the teakettle's humming seemed to skip a beat. I finally raised my head enough to look across the table at Dad.

Little ridges had formed between his eyes and he cocked his head to one side. He pursed his mouth as if trying to say something but no words came out. Finally he spoke in slow, deliberate words, "Jeffrey Nickerson, you—you were rude to Joe?" Trying hard to hold back the tears, I moved my head up and down.

"But—but why? And when? You hardly spoke to him all the time he was here."

"Well, he showed up down at the creek when I was watching the salmon. He had his gun and I thought he was going after the other swan. I was sitting out on that little island above the pool and he made some remark about me going to sleep and falling in. So, I just told him that even if I did, it would be none of his business."

"What did he say then?"

"Nothing. He just asked where you were and went on his way. He didn't tell you about it?" I asked.

"No." Dad picked up his fork and started to eat. My

appetite had vanished and I said, "Mind if I walk down to the lake?"

"No, but if you wait a bit, I'll go with you. We won't stay long though, because we have a long day ahead of us tomorrow."

"What are we going to do?"

"We're going to see Joe Nilchik."

10

This would almost be fun, I thought, if we were making the trip for any other reason. The day turned out clear, somewhat crisp in the early hours, but the trail was dry and easy to follow. I had the feeling that this whole thing was as hard on Dad as it was for me. I thought at first that he was making a mountain out of a mole hill, but I could tell by the way he plodded on ahead of me that he considered this serious business.

I rehearsed over and over in my mind what I'd say to Joe Nilchik. I just hoped he'd accept my apology and that he wouldn't think I was saying I was sorry just to please my father. What if, what if, what if? The words seemed to come out in rhythm with my steps and added worry to weariness as I tried to keep up with my dad's long strides. This was one lesson I knew I wouldn't forget.

The Alaskan evening sun was still high in the sky when we settled down in our bedrolls. I liked the coziness and security of knowing that Dad was in charge and I just had to believe that things would turn out all right.

"Dad, when you were a boy did you ever do or say anything you wished you hadn't, like I did to Joe?" I asked.

Dad didn't answer me right away and I heard him chuckling before he said, "I'm afraid so."

"What did you do?"

"Well, back when I was growing up on the farm, there used to be a tramp making the rounds each summer. He'd go from farm to farm, sleep in barns, and usually get invited into the farmhouse for breakfast. Everyone called him Papeeno and he was as much a part of the North Dakota summer as thunder showers and lightning.

"One time a buddy and I were riding on the back of a truck loaded with potatoes. Your grandfather was driving. We passed Papeeno on the road and after we got by, I picked up a potato and threw it at him—hit right in the top of the old hat he was wearing. Didn't really hurt him—he staggered a bit but kept on shuffling down the road. Well, that night your grandfather overheard my buddy and me laughing about what a good shot I was with a potato. He made us tell what happened."

"What'd he do about it?"

"He loaded me and my friend into the truck and we drove all over the countryside looking for Papeeno. We finally found him just getting ready to bed down in one of the neighbor's barns. I had to tell him I was sorry and the other kid apologized for laughing. Your grandfather then took him home with us and had him spend the night. He let him sleep in my bed and my buddy and I slept in the barn."

I laughed, trying to picture my dad throwing a potato at the tramp. "Well, hay's softer than this ground is," I said. "And at least you got to ride." Dad reached over, patted me on the arm and said goodnight.

When we broke camp the next morning Dad said, "You lead the way today. After all, it's your show." He winked at me. The trail was easy to follow, if rougher, with the morainal deposits of a glacier which snailed its way through hundreds of years ago. Often looking behind to make sure Dad was coming, I tried to set a steady pace with rest stops spaced out so we'd accomplish our goal of reaching fish camp by late afternoon. We stopped for a snack in the middle of the afternoon and I was encouraged when Dad said we only had about two more miles to go.

I felt a new springiness in my step and somehow what I had to do didn't seem as threatening as it had the day before. Dad was asking me to do something he'd had to do; he'd survived it and I could too. We rounded a fairly sharp curve in the trail and the next time I looked back Dad was nowhere in sight. I stopped to wait for him. He didn't show up so I retraced my steps and went looking. I called out to him but got no answer. That's strange, I thought, but soon discovered why.

Sprawled face down, Dad was lying in the middle of the trail. A small trickle of blood oozed out from a swelling on his forehead. Must have fallen and hit his head on one of the rocks, I figured, as I knelt beside him. Checking to see that he was breathing, I tried hard to remember what I'd learned when I worked for my first aid badge in Boy Scouts.

Removing his pack as gently as I could, I looked for the first aid kit he always carried. I placed a compress over the bleeding area, covered him with a sleeping bag and put my jacket under his head. I kept saying over and over, "Wake up, Dad, please, Dad, wake up." I felt alone and helpless. "Please, God, help my dad to be okay," I prayed. Huddling over him to check his breathing again, I felt a slight movement of his shoulders and a moment later he moved his head from one side to the other. "Come on, Dad, you're okay. Wake up and talk to me. Da-ad," I pleaded.

Finally, he opened his eyes, raised up on one elbow but quickly eased himself down again. Low groans encouraged me and I kept talking, "Please, Dad, don't go back to sleep." The next time he opened his eyes he said my name and I knew he was coming to.

"You don't look very comfortable, Dad. Can you turn over?" He made an effort but sank back down again. "My foot," he moaned. "Something's the matter with my foot."

"Which one?"

"Right one." Untying the laces on Dad's boot, I pulled it off as gently as I could. Dad groaned and I noticed the ankle had started to swell. "Do you think it's broken?" I asked.

"Don't know—feels like it. See if you can find a couple straight sticks for a splint."

I felt better already. Dad was talking, making sense, and even the prospect of having a broken foot seemed better than him lying there unconscious. I cut two pieces of wood and Dad told me to take the flannel liner out of the other sleeping bag, roll it up and put it under his foot and up each side of the leg. "Gotcha," I said and went about fixing the makeshift splints. "Looks like we're in business except I need something to tie with."

"Use the lace out of my boot and then double up some of the bandage strips from the kit," Dad suggested. I tried to be gentle but he shut his eyes tight and made a face when I fastened the splint on.

"Think we can turn you over now?" I asked. Dad said we could try. I spread out the other sleeping bag next to him and he raised himself up on his right elbow and with my help, over on his back. Dad let out a long slow breath and said he felt better already.

"I'm proud of you, Son. You're quite a medic." I got a better look at the head wound and noticed that it had stopped bleeding and the bandage was stuck to the swelled-up area. I left it there. Dad asked me to get a chunk of wood, or even a rock, to put under the sleeping bag under the bad foot. "Need to keep it elevated," he explained. He lay there with his eyes closed.

Satisfied that I'd done all I could for a while, I felt a chill go through my body and a sudden weakness settled over my entire being. Sitting on the ground, I folded my arms around my knees and stared at my feet. The immediate crisis was over; Dad was resting and things would turn out all right, I guessed. But what would happen now, I wondered. What if Dad couldn't walk and we'd have to stay here until he could? What if we ran out of food? I didn't have long to wait for an answer.

Dad opened his eyes, looked at me and said in a weak, apologetic voice, "I'm sorry, Jeff, but I don't think I'll be able to move for a while. You'll have to go on to fish camp alone and ask Joe to come help us."

11

Trying to picture in my mind how far two miles would be, I started down the trail after loosening the splint and putting some food and the rifle within Dad's reach. I know Dad hated to see me leave and he said a short prayer asking God to take care of me along the way. He told me to go until I came to the mouth of Tanada Creek and then follow the Copper down to fish camp, and that Joe would know what to do then.

Maybe Joe won't even want to help, I worried. Wouldn't exactly blame him—he'd had time to think about how snotty I'd been to him. But Joe wasn't all I thought about. Here I was—alone in the Alaskan wilderness, Dad was back on the trail with a broken foot, and what if a bear came along and he couldn't get away. I tried to focus my mind on the path ahead and not dwell on how scared I was. Sometimes the trail led close to the creek and I caught glimpses of salmon fins slithering through the water on their way to renewal and death. Trying to match their urgency, I walked faster until the roar in the distance let me know I was at least in earshot of the Copper River.

Stopping to listen, I heard something else besides the noise of the river. Sounding like some kind of engine, first it was real loud and then it would dwindle down to nothing. I thought I must be imagining things and kept on going until the steady drone of a motor convinced me that some kind of vehicle was ahead somewhere. It sounded like Grandpa's old farm tractor and when I came to the mouth of Tanada Creek, I looked off to the right just in time to see an odd-looking contraption coming down the old trail Dad called Batzel ... something or other.

Standing in the middle of the path, I waved my arms and the swamp buggy ground to a halt. The driver looked down at me from the cab of the rig. "Hi," he said, "something the matter?"

"It's my dad. He's back up the trail about two miles and I think he has a broken foot."

"What's your name?" the driver asked.

"Jeff Nickerson. My Dad's Larry Nickerson."

"Yah, I know him." He took his cap off, wiped his dusty forehead with the back of his hand and then put his cap back on. He looked around to the back of the vehicle and called to the boy now leaning out over the sideboards. "Jimmy, you go with this boy back to be with his daddy. I take Gramma to camp and come back with Joe."

"Thank you, thank you," I said. Jimmy jumped off the back of the buggy and we watched it growl its way down along the bank of the Copper River. Jimmy and I looked at one another, sizing each other up. Built like his dad, he was shorter than I, had shoulder length black hair and dark eyes. We headed up the trail walking side by side.

"My dad told me about you. I've already met your father and mother. I knew you were coming sometime soon. You sure got here at the right time."

"How did your daddy get hurt?" Jimmy asked in a

quiet, slightly-accented voice.

"Guess he tripped on a rock or something. Anyway, he fell and bumped his head and hurt his foot. Hope he's okay. I hated to leave him."

"My dad and Uncle Fred probably won't be too far behind us. They can come part way with the swamp buggy," Jimmy said. He took the lead when the trail narrowed and set a good pace, moving along with a special grace and seeming very much at home here in the wilderness. I felt safer having him along and I began to feel better about everything.

Noticing the Little League insignia on his cap when we stopped to rest, I asked, "You play baseball?"

Jimmy nodded. "You?"

"Some," I said. "I'm not very good at it but I like to pitch. I brought my glove and ball so I could practice this summer but Dad's been too busy so far."

"I like to pitch, too," Jimmy said. "Maybe we can work out."

"When we recover from this hike," I commented. "And I think we're getting close. I remember that clump of willows—when I went by them before I thought about Sven."

"You met Sven already?" Jimmy asked.

"He stayed with us for a few days. Wasn't feeling too well. But he improved and we got up one morning and he was gone," I said.

"Funny guy," Jimmy said. "He visits fish camp every year. Long hike. Sometimes I go with my daddy to his place in the winter with the snowmachine."

"Did he ever tell you his last name?" I asked.

"No, I guess not," Jimmy answered. "I know his

initials, though. He had Grandma make him a beaded belt one time. Wanted SSO on it. I remember it because I thought it should be SOS because he always needed help." We both laughed. I was beginning to like this friendly boy who seemed to share my happiness a few minutes later when we found Dad sitting up and looking better than when I'd left him.

"Didn't expect you this soon, Jeff. And Jimmy, look at you, you've grown a foot since I saw you two summers ago. Am I ever glad to see you two! Your father with you?" Dad asked, looking down the trail.

"He's coming with my uncle," Jimmy said.

"His uncle had to take his grandmother to camp first," I went on to explain. "We sure are lucky. Just when I got to the river, Jimmy and his Uncle Fred and his grandmother drove up in the swamp buggy."

"Then you haven't seen Joe yet, Jeff?" Dad asked. I shook my head, realizing that even a broken foot wasn't going to make him forget what had to be done.

Trying to change the subject, I said, "Looks like you're turning into a unicorn, Dad. That lump on your head looks like you're sprouting a horn. You took the bandage off."

"Guess it fell off during one of my naps. I slept quite a while—felt better when I woke up. You took good care of me, Son. Guess I'll have to recommend you for a merit badge in first aid."

"Don't you remember?" I reminded him. "I already have it. But right now, I'd like to work on my cooking badge—I'm starved. Anything left or did you eat it all?"

"There's stuff in the pack but we don't have time for a picnic. Here comes the rescue squad." It was a happy reunion.

"You had good doctor," Joe said after he and Fred examined the sore foot. Too embarrassed to look Joe in the face, I was nonetheless pleased with the compliment.

"Need to tie splint tighter," Fred said. "Think you can get up?" They each got on one side of Dad and helped him to stand.

"You guys make good crutches," Dad quipped, draping his long arms over their sturdy shoulders. Jimmy and I carried the packs and led the way.

When we reached the parked swamp buggy, Dad was obviously in great pain and I was relieved when Fred said he'd take him to the main road where he'd left his pickup and then on to the small hospital in Glennallen, 70 miles away.

"Can Jeff stay with us?" Jimmy asked his father.

"Sure, if it's okay with his daddy." I looked at Joe and then at Dad to see what he wanted me to do.

"He can stay," Dad said with no hesitation. It wasn't easy saying goodbye but Dad promised to send us a Caribou Clatter on the radio as soon as he found out about his foot. The men helped him into the cab and Fred started the noisy engine. Just as they took off, Dad cupped his hands around his mouth and yelled, "Remember Papeeno!"

12

"You boys sleep in that cache," Joe said after the fish-wheel had been checked for the last time and the other evening chores done. "Move stuff around to make room." I'd been curious about the little log building sitting on stilt-like legs and boasting a crude ladder made of peeled poles. Metal pieces that looked like old coffee cans were wrapped around the legs that supported the structure and gave it a half-decorated look.

"What are those cans there for?" I asked.

"Helps to keep the animals out—got lots of stuff in here, furs, food, everything."

"You ever sleep here before?"

"Lots of times."

"Reminds me of my tree house at home," I said, waiting for Jimmy to go up the ladder first.

"You ever sleep in your tree house?"

"Once in a while—when I can find someone to stay with me. My dad tried it once but his legs were too long and he got up in the middle of the night and went back into the house. Wonder how he's making out right now."

Despite the distractions of the evening activity around fish camp, I couldn't get Dad off my mind. I kept thinking about how I'd botched everything up and that it was really my fault that Dad got hurt. I felt guilty—and then there was the apology to Joe hanging over my head. There never seemed to be a right time to talk to him about it; we were never alone.

Tired as I was, I lay there awake long after Jimmy's even breathing let me know he was asleep. I wasn't used to the constant roar of the river and the raspy, creaking fishwheel. I'd put bug dope on my face to discourage the mosquitoes but their constant humming competed with the river talk.

Finally deciding I needed to go to the bathroom, I put my pants and shoes back on and crawled down the ladder, trying not to wake Jimmy. And since I still felt wide awake, I decided to go sit on the river bank and watch the fishwheel for a while.

I found the contraption fascinating and never tired of watching it dip its wire baskets into the muddy water and occasionally being rewarded by bringing up a wiggling fish. And I was beginning to like the long Alaskan days which never ended but pushed into the next with only a gentle dusk in between. Sitting here by myself in the half daylight, I could see why Dad was so hooked on Alaska.

I looked downriver and hoped that soon Jimmy and I could go exploring—even if it did mean going by the swan skin hanging on the smokehouse wall. I thought about the nesting trumpeter and wondered if it was still hanging in there without us being around to check on it every day.

Starting to get chilly, I decided I'd better get a jacket or go back to bed. Just as I began to leave the river bank I noticed a large object floating in the water upstream. Looks like a boat, I thought at first, but as it got nearer, I could see it was a large log and it was heading right for the fishwheel. I watched helplessly as the quick current pushed the log right into the upstream part of the raft holding the wheel. Swirling around awkwardly, a branch from the floating tree reached up and tangled itself in one of the baskets and stopped the wheel from turning.

Noticing that the whole thing was tugging hard at the wires which anchored the wheel, I realized that something had to be done. I ran to the tent and yelled for Joe. He stuck his head out of the tent. "There's a log caught in the fishwheel!" I yelled.

Not even stopping to dress his feet, Joe ran to the river bank, grabbed a long piece of wood and balancing himself on the sides of the box, tried to pry the log away from the raft. It wouldn't budge. "Get my axe from that smokehouse," he shouted. I was glad to have something to do besides stand there and watch. Joe took the axe and chopped away the branch caught in the wheel. This relieved some of the pressure but the upper wire was still straining on the tree it was fastened to and it looked like it could give way at any moment. Grabbing the wire, I pulled as hard as I could but was very relieved when Maggie joined me. Joe kept at his prying and seemed alarmed when the whole raft lurched sideways just as he gave a heavy push with the pole. Much to our relief, the big log moved away and spiraled along its marauding path downriver.

"Whew! Close one," Joe said as he hopped ashore, tightened the wire and wiped his brow, covered with sweat despite the chilliness of the evening. Maggie hurried to the tent to get something for Joe to dry off with and she brought me a small blanket to throw over my shoulders.

"I make tea," she said softly, showing that this time

was special and called for some sort of celebration.

"Bad luck to lose fishwheel," Joe explained as he and I stood together on the river bank, somehow not wanting to leave—as if we needed to stand guard for a spell. "No fish for family, no fish for dogs. Real bad luck to lose fishwheel. How come you see it?"

"Well, I couldn't sleep so I got up and decided to watch the wheel for a while. I was getting ready to go back to bed when I saw the log."

"Miss you daddy?" Joe asked. I nodded. "He'll be okay—tough guy. You tough too—hard to pull on that wire."

Maggie came with the tea and then went back into the tent. Joe sat on a stump and I sat on the ground nearby. "Your dad be proud when I tell him you save my fishwheel. Good thing you was here."

The wheel had resumed its rhythmic creaking and seemed all of a sudden to be grinding out a chorus of "Remember Papeeno, remember Papeeno, remember Papeeno." I knew what I had to do and this was the moment.

"Joe," I said, "Dad may be proud of me for helping save the fishwheel but he wasn't very proud of me the other day when I told him I'd been rude to you down by the creek because I thought you were coming to shoot the other swan. The reason we were coming here was so I could tell you I was sorry—I really am sorry. I know my dad was ashamed of me. I asked God to forgive me and now I'm asking you to do the same."

There was a long silence as if Joe was trying to make sense out of my long speech. I got up enough courage to glance at his dark face just as he stood and said, "You good boy. Better go to bed again—lots to do tomorrow."

"Thanks, Joe. Good night." Heading for the cache, I felt as if I had springs in my heels. An overwhelming sense of relief came over me, as if a big log had been removed from my back and tossed into the muddy, swirling water of the Copper.

13

Dad sent us a Caribou Clatter message from the radio station in Glennallen the day after he left with Fred. We were all glad when he said no bones were broken—that his injury was just a bad sprain and torn ligaments. The doctor wanted him to stay in town until the swelling went down and he was staying in the village with Fred. He ended the message with the words: "Tell Jeff I miss him. Remember Papeeno."

"Papeeno—what does Papeeno mean?" Jimmy asked. "Is that some kind of secret code?"

"You got it," I answered and glanced shyly at Joe who winked at me but said nothing. I wished there was some way I could let Dad know that I'd made my peace with Joe but the more I thought about it, the more I realized that maybe he did know. After all, he trusted me—even if I did let him down and disappoint him once in a while. I tried not to spend too much time worrying and was happy when a big run of salmon kept us all hustling.

In tune with the daily arrival of the fish in the wheel, life at camp had a special rhythm of its own. I helped Jimmy cut alder for the smokehouse, pack water from the small stream not too far from camp, feed the dogs, carry salmon from the wheel to where Maggie worked on them, and there were always buckets of scraps to be dumped into the river. After the chores were all caught up I liked to sit in the big tent and visit with Jimmy's

Grandma. When Joe had explained who I was, her wrinkled face with the scarred cheek had lit up and she kept saying over and over again, "Yah, yah, Larree, Larree." I enjoyed listening to her constant, soft Athabascan chatter although I couldn't understand what she was saying. Despite her failing eyesight, she kept busy sewing skins and making birch bark baskets laced with spruce root.

One day she held out a small piece of root and said, "*Xay, xay*, need *xay*."

"Grandma wants more spruce roots," Jimmy explained. "Want to go with me to find some?"

"Sure. Where do we go?"

"I'll show you. You got a knife?"

"It's in my pack," I said and went to the cache to get it. A twinge of homesickness hovered over me for a moment as I loosened my belt and slipped the end of it through the loop in the sheath. The knife and case had been Mom's parting gift to me—she'd even had my initials etched in the case: JON. My thoughts soon turned to other things as I followed Jimmy downriver.

Noticing the brightly beaded strap around Jimmy's waist, I said, "That's a real pretty belt you have. And that knife case, what's it made of?"

"Moose hide. Got it for my tenth birthday. Grandma made the belt. She used to do lots of beadwork but now she doesn't see too good. My mother made the knife holder and my daddy made the knife." He pulled it out of its case and passed it to me.

"Never saw one like this before—feels good in the hand," I said. The knife had a very narrow blade and a handle made of moose antler. The letters JON were etched into the handle. "JON—hey, your initials are the same as mine," I exclaimed. "What's your middle name?"

"Orville. Yours?"

"Olsen. Funny, huh?" I passed the knife back to him. "Skinny blade," I commented.

"Good for skinning muskrats," Jimmy said, replacing the knife in its case without a break in his confident stride.

"How come we're going way down here for the roots? Aren't those spruce trees up by the camp?" I asked.

"Wrong kind," Jimmy replied. "We call that kind swamp spruce. Grandma always gets it from the tall, straight spruce." We finally left the river trail and headed inland about a quarter of a mile. Stopping by a clump of willows, Jimmy took out his knife, cut off a sturdy stick and sharpened the end of it. "We need sharp sticks to dig with," he explained. I cut one, too.

As we approached a stand of spruces, I noticed that some of the brush had disappeared and the woods looked like a park with the tall pitchy trees reaching up out of the mossy floor. "We need to get long straight pieces about this thick," Jimmy said as he put his thumb and finger close together. "And they need to be a little bit red, too. Just keep digging until you find some. Start out quite far from the tree trunk." I watched to see how he did it. I pulled too hard on the first one and it broke but I soon got the hang of it. It was sort of fun and I liked the pungent smell of the fresh roots as we stripped off the thin outer bark and coiled up the long strips.

"Let's take a rest," Jimmy said and he pulled a piece of smoked salmon out of his pocket and handed me a chunk. I was beginning to like the stuff and although it was dark and dry on the outside, the inside was juicy, tasty and filling. The saltiness made us thirsty and Jimmy suggested we go get a drink from a small creek nearby. "Same one that runs by camp," he explained. "We'll leave the roots here."

We hadn't gone very far when Jimmy stopped and motioned me to do the same. He pointed up ahead to an open area where a little brown animal rested on a bed of moss. "Looks like a calf," I whispered.

"Moose calf," Jimmy murmured. "Not very old." The calf lay still except for the constant flicking of the ears. I started to step up ahead to get a better look but Jimmy grabbed my sleeve and shook his head at me. "We better watch out—that old cow's around here somewhere."

We didn't have to guess where because the crashing of brush behind us let us know we'd better get out of there fast. "Run!" Jimmy yelled and led the way around the calf. "Quick—up that tree!" I grabbed a bottom branch, pulled myself up with a boost from Jimmy, then reached down to help him. We made it just in time—a moment later the angry cow moose snorted by with her ears laid back and the top of her neck looking like a punk hairdo. She disappeared off to the left of the tree.

"Whew! That was close," I panted. "Do you think she knows we're here?"

"She knows we're here somewhere. She could smell us."

"Now what do we do?" I asked, not really expecting an answer. We climbed a bit higher but the thicker branches kept us from going too far.

"Better try to make yourself comfortable," Jimmy said. "Looks like we'll be here for a while." Copying him, I started breaking little dry branches off a larger limb in trying to make a smooth place to sit.

"Hope we don't have to stay here too long," I said. "Almost as bad as sitting on a porcupine."

"Well, we might be sitting on a moose if she shakes us out of this tree," Jimmy said—jokingly, I hoped. We kept listening and watching for telltale movements around us. First we'd hear a noise in one direction and then another. At one point we caught a glimpse of the cow not too far from our tree.

"Sure is a big animal," I said. "This is the closest I've ever been to a live moose."

"You been close to a dead one?" Jimmy asked.

"Not really—at least not a whole one. Grandpa used to have an old moose head hanging in the living room at the farm. Grandma moved it out after Grandpa died—called it an old dust catcher.

"My grandma wouldn't want an old moose head hanging in the living room either. She'd rather eat it," Jimmy said.

"Moose head's good to eat?" I asked.

"Sure—best part, especially the nose. All the old people like that best."

"Well, my grandma used to make hog head cheese so I guess there's no difference. Moose head—pig head."

"Except we don't hang pig heads on our wall," Jimmy remarked. We both laughed.

"Speaking of heads," I whispered, "look." The cow moose stepped out from behind a clump of bushes and began browsing on the fresh willow leaves. She seemed calmer than before but kept turning her head and looking back. We soon saw why. Her calf wobbled along behind her and kept trying to nurse, its stub of a tail flicking back and forth. The mother finally stopped pruning the bushes and nuzzled the little animal while it ate. All of a sudden, as if sensing danger, the cow took off on a trot with the little one following on its unsure, gangly legs.

"First time I ever saw one eat off the mother," Jimmy said in a hushed voice that let me know he was just as awed as I was at what we'd just witnessed. We sat quietly on our perches until we could no longer hear crashing in the brush.

"I think she's gone," Jimmy said finally, and I followed him down out of the tree. We listened again and hearing nothing, headed back in the direction of where we'd left our spruce roots.

"I forgot all about being thirsty," I said.

"Me, too," Jimmy answered. "Let's go home."

14

Waking to the sound of drizzling rain the next morning, Jimmy and I stayed in our cozy bedrolls, not wanting to venture out into the damp, chilly morning. I thought about Dad and wondered how he was doing. I worried about how he'd get back to the cabin with his bum foot. Jimmy finally poked me and asked, "What's the matter—you're so quiet."

"Just thinking about my dad, is all."

"Maybe we'll get a clatter from him today," Jimmy said as he sat up, leaned over and opened the makeshift door enough to look out at the soggy day. "Boy, look at the fog out there—can't hardly see the river."

"Well, it hasn't dried up because I can hear it," I said.

"I hear something else out there, too. My dad's talking to someone—man's voice." We both listened but the rain on the cache roof muffled the sounds and we couldn't tell who it was. Our curiosity aroused, we dressed quickly, climbed down the ladder and hustled toward the big tent. Jimmy ducked inside but I stopped at the entrance, my eye caught by the familiar-looking pack leaning up against a nearby tree. Looks like Sven's, I thought.

And Sven's it was. When I entered the tent a hearty, "Hey there, young feller," greeted me. Hunching my shoulders as I usually did when I felt a bit shy, I reached out and took the old prospector's outstretched hand. Gnarled fingers wrapped around mine and he said, "Joe told me about your Pa. He'll be okay." I nodded, wondering what else Joe had told him.

Sven explained that he'd come back to the cabin at the lake and had stayed overnight, thinking that Dad and I would show up. He knew we weren't in the mountain area because we would have stopped in to see him at his place. He'd headed downstream and just kept coming when he didn't find us.

"Broke camp early this mornin'," he said. "Rain started pelting in on me. Didn't think it'd start till about noon. Knew it was a-comin' 'cause the old knees was stiffenin' up." Joe made room for him on the bench closest to the stove.

Maggie made tea and a big pot of oatmeal. I was having a hard time getting used to canned milk on my cereal but on this cool, damp morning anything would have tasted good. Jimmy and I hurried through our outside morning chores and were content to sit in the crowded tent and listen to the men talk. The rhythm of rain on the roof and the murmuring of the fire in the Yukon stove made me sleepy and I leaned back, half lying down, and with my head propped up on one arm. Jimmy sat beside me.

Grandma stayed in her special corner with her sewing things neatly stacked on the shelves fastened to the log framework which supported the tent. She'd been pleased with the spruce roots we'd brought her and kept saying, "*Deniigi, deniigi,*" when Joe explained to her about our encounter with the moose. During a lull in the conversation, she pulled a brown fur hat out of one of her baskets and passed it to Sven. He looked it over carefully, petting the fur, tying the flaps on top and then untying them, and finally putting the cap on his head. With his half-toothed grin, he looked around for everyone's approval. He seemed different from the Sven who'd walked out on us a few weeks before without even saying goodbye.

"Looks like an Ewok," Jimmy whispered to me and I nodded.

"Nice beaver hat," Joe said as Sven got up off his seat and lumbered through the tent flaps. I had a hard time to equate the neatly-made hat with the fuzzy, brown animal Dad and I had watched that magical evening which now seemed so long ago. I wondered what a beaver would think about part of himself spending years atop an old man's tangled head.

Sven was still wearing the hat when he came back into the tent moments later. Carrying a bundle of fur pieces tied together, he undid them and spread them out in front of Jimmy's grandma. She picked up one piece after another, smoothed out the grayish-brown fur, and examined them carefully. Scanning the batch as if counting, she finally stashed the whole bunch on her crowded shelf.

"Grandma makes me mukluks out of that kind," Jimmy said.

"What is it?" I asked.

"Caribou leg—makes good winter boots. I like to wear them when I mush dogs. They don't weigh much and I can run fast in them."

Sven sat holding his new hat, obviously pleased with the trade. "Guess I won't freeze my ears next time it's 40 below and I'm caught out in a blizzard," he remarked and he pushed back the unkempt hair on one side of his head and exposed the shriveled top of his ear. I couldn't imagine anyone being that cold, especially when the tent suddenly seemed so hot.

"Looks like rain stopping," Joe said and he got up and went outside. Jimmy and I followed but Sven stayed in by the fire.

"How long is Sven going to stay?" I asked Joe.

"We talk about it this morning. Said he'd stay till we hear from your daddy." We didn't have long to wait. The noon Caribou Clatters brought the welcome message— the doctor had given Dad a good report on his foot and he'd arranged for a bush pilot to fly him back into the lake as soon as the weather cleared, hopefully by the weekend. He asked if Joe could take me back to the cabin.

Joe explained that Sven had already volunteered to go back with me. I could hardly contain my excitement. Dad was coming home, I'd have a chance to spend time with Sven, and things were going to be okay again. And when the clouds scurried off to the east in early afternoon and the sun came out in earnest, Sven decided we should leave. He seemed as excited as I was.

"We'll git a few miles in today," he said. "This is Thursday, ain't it?" My legs ain't as long as your dad's but if we plug away at it, we kin git there maybe before he does." He seemed charged with a new source of energy and pranced around as if the pains in his legs had been blown away with the scudding clouds. Maggie gave us a good supply of smoked salmon and everyone looked sad when we shouldered our packs and started out on the long trek. I hated to leave Jimmy and was cheered when Joe said, "Me and Jimmy come see you in a couple weeks."

15

Like migrating salmon, Sven and I headed upstream, hoping to race Dad back to the cabin. I found it easy to keep up with Sven who shuffled along at a steady pace, occasionally looking back to check on me. Pointing out the place where Dad had tripped, I explained how I'd gone to get Joe for help, only to meet Fred and the swamp buggy at the mouth of Tanada Creek. Funny how things had worked out, I thought. First of all, there was help closer than we'd expected. And then Sven had showed up just at the right time to go back to the cabin with me. I guessed that Someone was really watching over us—good things to balance the bad. That's what Grandpa Nickerson used to tell me.

We didn't talk much as we trekked along, Sven needing all his breath just to keep going. When we stopped to have a smoked salmon snack, I asked him if he'd seen the swan back at the lake.

"Shore did. She was on the nest as pert as can be."

"When do you think the eggs will hatch?"

"Should be soon—takes little over a month," Sven replied.

"We were sure worried when she lost her mate. Guess Joe ended up with it."

"Whatever makes you think that?" Sven asked, wrinkling up his forehead and looking at me real squinty-eyed.

"Well, the first time we were at fish camp, I saw what

looked like a swan skin hanging on the smokehouse wall," I explained. "We were quite sure it was our swan and I thought Joe had shot it even though he said he found it dead up along the creek."

"If Joe said he found it dead, he found it dead," Sven said with a tone that let me know I shouldn't question it further. The old guilt feelings started to creep in again and I decided to blurt out the whole story of my sassy remark to Joe and that was the reason we'd gone back to see him. Sven listened and didn't say anything but I detected a slight hint of amusement as he kept pulling on his scraggly beard.

"Looks like ya took yer punishment like a man," Sven finally said. "And Joe told me how ya saved the fishwheel."

"Well, I was glad I did something right for a change. Seems like I've done my share of botching things up this summer. You ever do anything you were real sorry for?" I asked, hoping for a Papeeno-like story similar to Dad's.

The look on Sven's face told me I shouldn't have asked such a question and that invisible curtain of gloom seemed to drop out of nowhere, shutting out that special feeling of comradeship I'd felt just moments before.

The mood didn't change as we set up camp about halfway between the Copper and the beaver dam and went about our evening chores. Sven crawled into the lean-to shelter long before the sun went down but I sat up, feeding the campfire green willows in hopes that the mosquitoes would move on. Somehow I felt very much alone. Sven hadn't said much and I tried to think back to our conversation along the trail and what I might have said to send him off to wherever he'd retreated.

Finally letting the fire burn down, I crawled into my bedroll beside Sven and lay awake listening to the evening sounds of a scolding Canada jay and the incessant gurgling of the creek not too far way. Every once in a while, a splash in the stream reminded me of the drama taking place close by and I dreamily imagined myself riding on top of a huge king salmon and trying to turn it around so it would head back downstream.

Frequent splashing was still going on the next morning when we broke camp. "Must be a new run comin' in—seem to come in spurts," Sven said. He was a bit more talkative than he'd been the evening before but I sensed a restlessness in the old man. He seemed eager to get going again. I think we both felt a sense of urgency in trying to get back to the cabin before Dad flew in. And when we finally reached our destination the middle of the next morning, it was soon apparent that we'd won the race.

We were both tired but I was excited about the fact that Dad could arrive at any moment, and I kept imagining that I heard a plane off in the distance. I checked on the swan which was still sitting patiently on the nest, packed water, and busied myself with little chores around the cabin.

Thinking that perhaps it would make the time go by faster, I finally took my fish pole and headed for the grayling pool. I asked Sven if he wanted to go but he just shrugged his shoulders and murmured, "Guess not."

The pool was full of salmon milling around so I decided not to fish but sat and watched a while, noting the deep red of the fresh run. I never tired looking at the swirling splashes of color as they flopped out of the water once in a while, as if trying to see what was up there.

Plodding back to the cabin sometime later, I suddenly realized how worn out I really felt and could appreciate more how Sven must be feeling. He'd set a mean pace the last few miles as if he'd suddenly shifted to automatic pilot and nothing was going to change it. I thought about how kind he'd been to me despite his moodiness and that I really needed to thank him before Dad got back so he'd know I'd thought of it all by myself. Despite my good intentions, however, I didn't get the chance.

Glancing towards the lake as I approached the cabin, I caught sight of a lonely figure, stooped and struggling as it moved slowly through the muskeg and finally disappeared into the heavier brush at the head of the lake. Maybe he just went to check on the swan, I kidded myself, knowing full well that he wouldn't be back.

A feeling of great loneliness hung over me as evening came with no sign of my dad. I got all excited when a plane flew over in the late afternoon, circled the area and then headed off without landing. Trying to work off my disappointment, I busied myself straightening up the shelves, rearranging supplies and wiping off the table and windowsill. Standing back to admire my work, I noticed that something seemed to be missing from the window shelf. I had a hard time figuring out why the small sill suddenly looked so bare, and then it hit me—the family picture wasn't there. I looked around the cabin but couldn't find it and decided that Dad must have put it in his pack when we headed for fish camp.

I really wanted to walk down to the lake but somehow felt that I should stay close to the cabin, as if I might be expecting a telephone call. I sat on a stool by the table and thought I'd write a few notes about my observations of the swan but the light grew dimmer as the evening wore on. Although I'd watched Dad light the gas lantern many times, I didn't feel comfortable trying it myself. I moved over to the edge of the bottom bunk and finally leaned back and half dozed off. I couldn't figure out why Sven had left me here alone and not waited until Dad returned. Maybe it was all a bad joke and my dad wasn't coming back and Sven wasn't going to be coming back and I'd never see Joe or Jimmy again and I'd be left here in the wilds to fend for myself. My imagination romped out of control through shoulder-high clumps with bears, wolves and an old cow moose behind each one. It seemed that the whole world had gone somewhere and left me behind.

Lying there in a half-dazed state, I didn't hear the footsteps approaching outside the cabin, and when a familiar voice called out, "Anybody home?" I thought I was dreaming. It wasn't until the door squeaked open and Dad limped in that I realized it wasn't a dream and my nightmare was over. Grinning broadly, he walked over to the bunk, handed me a flat package and said, "Here, I brought you a pizza."

16

No pizza party was ever more enjoyed than the one Dad and I shared in the little cabin in the wilds of Alaska on the night he returned from Glennallen. Dad explained that he'd flown over the lake earlier but noticed that the swan was on her nest and didn't want to disturb her. So, he'd asked the pilot to land at Copper Lake and he'd hiked in from there. It'd taken him quite a while but he'd made it and I was there to greet him and things were going to be okay.

I just shook my head at his even wanting to try the hike with his bum foot. "And you carried the pizza all the way," I marveled. "Wish Jimmy was here to have some—he told me it's his favorite food."

Stretching out his lanky frame on the bunk and allowing me to prop up his leg, Dad asked, "Had a good time at fish camp, did you?"

"Sure did."

"And how about, uh?" Dad started to say but didn't finish when I bobbed my head up and down with a little extra push from my body. "Great, I had a feeling it was all settled," he continued.

I just about bubbled over trying to tell him everything about fish camp and the trek back with Sven. "By the way," I asked, "did you see Sven anywhere when you flew over? He left not too long after we got here. I thought he'd at least spend the night or wait until you came."

Dad shook his head. "Guess he figured you were smart enough to take care of yourself. Don't worry about him. He'll show up one of these days again when we least expect him..." Dad's voice trailed off to a mumble and I suddenly realized he'd fallen asleep. I crawled up into my own bunk and the cozy warmth I felt was not from the bedroll but from an invisible blanket woven together with safety, love and a special feeling of thankfulness.

And I could tell that Dad was thankful, too, when he prayed before we ate the next morning. But I was somewhat puzzled when he ended his prayer by asking God to help us face the special challenges of the day; I thought our challenges were all behind us.

"Guess I'll play invalid for a few days and let you pamper me. Doctor said I should take it easy for a while."

"That long hike yesterday probably didn't do your foot a favor," I said. "Can't believe you did that—and carrying a pizza, too."

Dad shrugged his shoulders. "Well, son, you do what you have to do. By the way, I called your mother and sister a couple times when I was in Glennallen."

"How're they doing?"

"Okay, I guess. Said they missed us. I told Sis you had a present for her."

"Hope you didn't tell her what it was. She'd probably quit feeding my dog," I laughed. Dad didn't seem to share my joke and I noticed a sudden look of sadness in his face. The telltale frown lines deepened and his head moved slightly from one side to another. "Something wrong?" I asked. "Your foot hurting?"

"No, my foot's okay," Dad said softly. "Son, I wish I didn't have to tell you this—but Tippy died. A truck hit her." I looked at Dad to make sure he wasn't kidding, knowing full well that he would have no part of such a cruel joke. His anguished look told me he was indeed telling the truth.

"But how'd she get out of the fence?" I asked.

"Dug a hole, I guess."

"Bet it wouldn't have happened if I'd been there. Should have stayed home in the first place—we'd all be better off." I stomped out of the cabin, slamming the door so hard it popped open again. Trying to come to grips with this bad news, I wandered aimlessly around outside the cabin for a while and then meandered down the trail leading to the lake.

Clenching my fist, I struck out at nothing in particular and fought to keep the tears back. Sadness soon replaced my anger, however, and when I realized I was fighting a losing battle, I hunkered down on a tussock and let myself go. I'd had a hard time coping with the events of the past few weeks and I'd tried to be brave but now it seemed that all the pent-up feelings let loose and I couldn't do a thing about it. I cried. I cried for the missing swan, I cried for my dad, I cried for Sven—mostly I cried for Tippy. I couldn't figure out how things could change so fast. Last night when Dad and I sat eating pizza, it seemed that nothing could invade the cozy happiness we shared. And now this.

Finally gaining control, I wiped my nose on my sleeve and tried to ward off the jillion mosquitoes buzzing around me despite the brightness of the day. I stood up and looked back towards the cabin. Dad was standing in the doorway. Not quite ready to go back, I headed on towards the lake. Reaching the shore, I followed along the path, hoping to see the swan. The nest was empty.

I was puzzled because Dad had said the swan was on the nest the day before and I'd seen it not long after Sven and I got back to the cabin. Disappointment settled in over my already depressed spirit and I slowly retraced my steps along the water's edge. Just before coming to the place where the trail took off, I noticed a flash of white at the other end of the lake. I stopped, squinted and took a good look to make sure I was really seeing what I thought I was seeing.

"Well, would you look at that?" I said aloud. Gliding along in gentle circles, a snowy swan led a parade of three small gray fluffs. I watched spellbound, and then hurried up the path. Long before reaching the cabin, I started calling for Dad. He met me in the doorway.

"Guess what? The swans hatched—three of them! But they all moved to the other end of the lake."

"They often move shortly after hatching," Dad explained. "They won't go very far—at least not until they get a few more feathers."

"Wish we could let Sven know they hatched," I said.

"We'll be going right by his place in a couple weeks," Dad said. He turned and followed me into the cabin. "By the way, I noticed how neat everything was on the shelves. The whole place sure looks good to me today."

"Well, I tried to keep busy while I was waiting for you. It was pretty lonely here after Sven took off."

"I know what you mean. I used to mind it the most when I'd get back after a few days at a study plot. Coming back to an empty cabin is the pits. I used to sit and stare at the family picture and imagine what it would be like to have you all here with me."

"Speaking of the family picture, do you have it in your pack?" I asked.

"No," he replied. "I thought maybe you'd moved it." I shook my head.

17

"Hard to believe those swans have changed so much in two weeks. Hope we find Sven so we can tell him the good news," I said. We had stopped to rest along the shores of Copper Lake and were surprised to find that the swan and her brood of three had moved in there.

"She's taking good care of her babies," Dad remarked. "They had quite a hike between the two lakes. It's a wonder a hungry fox or a beady-eyed hawk hadn't gobbled them up." I gave Dad a disgusted look, hoping of course that he was just teasing.

"They sure look funny going bottoms-up in the water—the mother looks like a miniature iceberg."

"Well, that giant iceberg in the distance is where we're headed so we'd better move along," Dad said, pointing to the snow-capped peak ahead.

I had sensed Dad's restlessness the past few weeks, and the planning and packing for this trip had found him excited and eager to get going. He'd explained that we'd swing by Sven's cabin the third day out and then head for the hills and the plateau area the following day.

"What if Sven isn't there?" I asked.

"We'll stay anyway," he'd replied.

On the morning of the third day I had that funny feeling in the pit of my stomach just like I used to get when we took trips to Grandpa Nickerson's farm. It always seemed to take forever to get there. I think Dad was as eager as I was to have a night when we wouldn't have to set up camp.

Approaching a small, clear creek about mid-morning, Dad pointed to a clump of trees upstream. "Sven's place is right in the middle of that spruce grove," he said. "We'll follow Mineral Creek here on this side. He has a little footbridge which crosses close to his cabin."

"Those trees sure are a lot bigger than the ones around our place," I remarked. "Looks like they're the only tall ones around, though."

"They are," Dad said. "You'll like Sven's place. He keeps all the brush cleaned out and it looks just like a park. Has a nice cabin, too."

"Wow! This bridge is wobbly," I remarked a bit later as I followed Dad across the logs which spanned the stream. I couldn't resist the temptation to bounce a bit but quit when I almost lost my balance. I quickly forgot about the bridge, however, as we followed the path leading to the cabin.

"This place makes ours look like a doghouse," I said. The sturdy cabin with the now-familiar sod roof seemed very much at home under some of the tallest spruces I'd seen since fish camp. The most welcome sight of all, however, was the smoke lazily wisping its way out of the smokestack.

"He's here," Dad said and then called out, "Anybody home?" The door opened and a grinning Sven greeted us.

"I figgered you guys'd show up one of these days. How's the foot?" Leading us into the large, neat room, he said, "I'll put some water on fer tea." I was amazed at the change in Sven. Neatly combed hair and beard had replaced the unkempt, bedraggled look and it almost seemed that the old man stood straighter than usual.

"This sure is a nice cabin, Sven," I said. "Did you build it?"

"Nope. Some guy moved in here in the early '40s. Thought he'd mine the creek but the guv'ment shut down all the gold minin' durin' the war. He asked me to stay here and look out fer the place. I 'spected him back in '45 when they decided it was okay to mine again but he never showed up. Been here almost forty years now waitin' fer him to come. Don't reckon he'll be back."

"Looks like you've taken good care of the place," I said.

"I keep workin' on it. The roof's a problem and I've had to put new logs around the bottom a few times. Ain't as strong as I used to be, so don't know what I'll do if they rot out again." He busied himself around the stove and getting the tea ready while Dad brought him up-to-date on what had gone on since we'd last seen him. He thanked Sven for accompanying me back to fish camp.

"And guess what?" I interrupted. "The swans hatched—three of them—and the whole family moved to Copper Lake."

"Ya don't say!" Sven answered, obviously pleased. "Guess I'll have to hike over and take a look at 'em— make sure she's bringin' 'em up right." He paused. "Ain't been doin' much hikin' lately. Hung perty close to home the past coupla weeks."

"Looks like you've been busy with diamond willow," I remarked, noting the neatly-peeled and sanded sticks leaning against the wall in the corner. "I sure like that table with the willow legs. What's the top made of?"

"Spruce burl—cut it off'n a tree a few years back. Had to let it dry a coupla years, then it took me another year to get it sanded the way I wanted it."

"How're the legs fastened on?"

"Jest fit 'em in like pegs—gouged out holes with a knife."

"Must have taken a long time," I said.

"Well, I got plenty of that," Sven answered.

"Mom would like a table like that, wouldn't she, Dad?" I said. "She likes old wooden things."

"She sure does," Dad replied. "Has them all over the place."

"I know. I remember the time I was playing with the hand-carved wooden swan candleholders she has. I dropped one and she thought I'd broken it. She sent me to my room and then came in and hugged me when she found out it was okay."

"Well, it was one of her most-prized pieces. Used to belong to your Grandma Olsen. She gave them to your mother as a gift on the day you were born. They both cried." Dad stood up and headed for the door. "Let's bring in our packs," he said. I followed him out.

"What's with Sven all of a sudden? He got that wide-eyed look when we were talking and then acted like we weren't even there," I said.

"Yeah, I noticed it, too. Let's try to ignore it," Dad sighed.

With rifle in hand, Sven appeared at the door just as Dad and I were going in. "Make yerselves to home," he muttered without looking at us. "I'll go git us a rabbit fer supper."

"We've got..." I started to say but quit when Dad gave me that special look of his that means I should keep my mouth shut. We watched as Sven disappeared into the brush beyond the spruce grove.

"Where's the guest room?" I asked.

"I always bunk on this side," Dad said as he placed his pack on the right at the back of the room.

"Boy, this is real uptown with two sets of bunks," I said.

"Yup, and Sven always keeps everything as neat as it is right now. I've shown up here when he had no idea I was around and the place always looks good."

"I sure like all the things he's made. That moose antler chair would take a prize at the fair." I wandered around the room looking at everything. Antler pegs dotted the four huge logs which spanned the room and held an assortment of tools and gadgets. The real windows on the two sides and the front of the cabin let in lots of light. Well-worn plywood formed a solid base to walk on. The kitchen corner with its neat shelves seemed rather bare; a few blackened pots hung in a row above a wide counter. "Sven doesn't seem to have many supplies," I remarked.

"Probably doesn't," Dad said.

"What if he runs out?"

"Oh, he'll make out—as long as he can hunt. He pretty much lives off the land. He's probably got meat in his permafrost pit outside. He used to make a couple trips a year to Chistochina, but now he depends on Joe to bring him some staples in the winter."

"Could we give him some of our stuff?"

"He'd be too proud to take it. He's lived so long fending for himself that it embarrasses him to take favors from anyone."

"Well, he sure is a puzzle. Don't know why he'd go off to find a rabbit when he had meat in his cooler."

"Guess he just wanted to get off by himself for a while." Dad shrugged his shoulders as if dismissing the prospect of trying to figure out Sven's actions. "Think I'll take a little rest and put my foot up for a while," he said.

"And I think I'll go outside and look around."

"Good idea," Dad said as he climbed into the bunk and put the bedroll under his foot. I went outside and walked around under the trees. A short way from the spruce grove was a cleared area with the usual cache sitting in the middle. The top of the cache sat on a platform supported by posts with big upside down cans on each one. Just like at fish camp, I thought—must be frustrating for the squirrels. I resisted the temptation to put the ladder in place and crawl up and explore inside.

Walking past some freshly-split logs close to the cabin, I decided to pile them up for Sven. The task soon finished, I thought I might try some splitting. Picking up the single-bit axe, I headed for the chopping block, well-worn and grooved as if it had been worked over by the beavers. I found the logs hard to split with their uneven grain and tangle of knots. Sven must be stronger than he looks, I thought, struggling with a tough piece which looked like someone had tried to wring it out while it was growing. After splitting a couple of toughies, I picked up a smaller straighter-grained stick. Raising the axe high over my head, I came down on the block with full force. It missed the middle but quickly found its way through the edge of the stick, glanced off the chopping block and settled blade-down on my left foot.

Stunned for a moment, I removed the axe and noticed that it had cut through my hiking boot. I felt a warm, liquid sensation inside my shoe and suddenly realized I'd cut myself. I hobbled towards the door just as Sven came into sight from the direction of the creek. Instead of a rabbit, he carried a string of grayling. I waited for him to catch up.

"Guess I hurt my foot," I said, pointing to my boot and noticing that blood was beginning to ooze through the cut.

"Looks like ya done a good job of it, son," Sven said with obvious concern in his voice. He opened the door and continued, "Let's go in and take a look at it."

Dad had apparently dropped off to sleep but raised himself up on one elbow when the door opened. I pointed to my foot Jumping up, Dad gently removed the boot while Sven stirred up the coals and put some water on to heat.

"Cut kind of deep there, Jeff," Dad said in a low voice. I felt like I was going to pass out and didn't object when Dad half carried me to the bed. He got his kit out of the pack and placing a compress over the wound, held it there to try to control the bleeding. When that didn't seem to stop it much, he placed the heel of his hand on my groin and that helped.

Looking down at the bloody mess my foot had become, I felt myself slipping away but I tried to fight the queasy feeling I always got at the sight of blood. I closed my eyes and the next thing I knew Dad and Sven were both standing by the bunk and Dad was putting some horrible smelling stuff up to my nose. Sven mopped my forehead with a cool, damp cloth and crooned, "There,

there, my boy."

It took a while for me to get my wits about me again and realize what had happened. My foot was one big bundle of bandage and when I tried to raise myself, Dad shook his head and motioned me to lie down.

"But I need to go to the bathroom," I protested.

"Sorry, buddy," Dad replied, "we'll have to fix you up with a tin can."

I lay in the bunk half-dozing while Sven bustled around and cooked the fish and Dad fixed some soup from a dried mix in our supplies. They wouldn't let me get up to eat but propped me up so it wasn't too awkward. "I should get well real fast with all the attention I'm getting," I said, but all of a sudden it occurred to me that once again I'd put a crimp in Dad's plans. I turned my head toward the wall and fought back the tears.

18

I woke early the next morning to find Dad rearranging our packs. Raising myself up, I threw the covers back but was soon reminded of the events of the day before. I carefully moved my feet and let them hang over the edge of the bunk.

Dad got up off the floor and walked over to my bed. "How're you doing there, old buddy?" he asked. "Better not try to stand yet." He checked the bandage and decided not to disturb it. "Looks like it hasn't bled anymore," he said. "That's good."

"Can I get up?" I asked.

"No, Sven and I think you should lay low for a couple of days so it won't start bleeding again."

"You two ganging up on me, huh?" I said, examining Dad's face and trying to figure out how everyone was going to cope with this new dilemma.

Dad sat on the floor next to my bunk and said, "Sven would be happy to have you stay here with him while I go do the study plot. I'll be gone for about six days if all goes well, and your foot should be fairly well healed by then."

Feeling as low as a tromped-on toad, I shook my head and settled back down and lay there staring at the bottom of the top bunk. "Water's hot," Sven said and Dad handed him a package of powdered chocolate milk mix. He bustled about, mixed the drink and was soon standing by my bed. "Here, son," he said. "This oughta perk ya up." He set the tin cup on the floor. "Yer gonna be jest fine," he continued. He had a tenderness in his voice which I'd never noticed before and he seemed to be enjoying his new role as nursemaid even if I was having a hard time dealing with it.

"Thanks," I said as I took the steaming drink. "Sorry to be such a bother." I never did like having anyone fussing over me. I wiggled my ankle and it hurt so I thought perhaps Sven and Dad were right and I should stay off it for a while. Sipping my drink and watching Dad finish packing, I thought I detected a slight hint of disappointment in his face as he wrestled the heavy pack to the door and made some remark about building up his muscles.

Walking back to me, he said, "I've left all your stuff here and I've taken only what food I'll need. I'm leaving the rest. You and Sven eat it up so we won't have to pack it home." He winked at me. "And don't worry about me, Jeff. My foot feels stronger today and I'll take it easy." He put his hand on my shoulder. "You do what Sven tells you—and no shenanigans!"

I grinned. "Fat chance for shenanigans. I'm sorry, Dad. Seems like I've spent the whole summer so far being sorry for one thing or another."

"There, there, now. Let's not think about things we can't change. You'll be up and about in a few days and perhaps Sven will show you his special grayling hole. He'll let you catch as many as you can, too. You still make pickled grayling, Sven?" Sven nodded.

The old man seemed almost pleased at the prospect of my staying with him for a few days. He followed Dad out the door and I could hear the murmur of voices for a few moments as the two chatted. A thump on the wall outside the cabin let me know Dad was on his way.

Carrying an armful of wood, Sven came back into the cabin and stoked the fire. "How about some flapjacks? Yer dad and I ate with the birds this mornin'."

"Okay," I said. "Just a couple of small ones. I'm not very hungry." I raised up out of my slump and watched Sven move from counter to stove as he fixed the breakfast. He half whistled and half hummed as he moved about. There was a perkiness about him this morning as if he'd been charged with a new kind of vigor.

I felt awkward eating breakfast in bed and Sven seemed to sense it because he left me alone after announcing he was going to get some water. Not feeling much like eating, I picked at my food and then settled back and lay there with my eyes closed, trying to picture Dad out on the trail somewhere, alone. He'd talked so much about this special plot. He'd explained about the gradual climb to the plateau area where the plot was located, and how beyond that were sharp cliffs and crags rising several thousand feet and providing homes for the beautiful white Dall sheep. I'd looked forward to seeing these unusual northern animals in their own habitat and not just as a stuffed trophy in a showroom.

I flexed my sore foot and thought it wasn't quite as stiff as when I first woke up. Guess it wouldn't hurt to dangle it over the side, I thought, but changed my mind when I heard Sven returning. He carried not only the bucket of water but also a couple lengths of fresh-cut diamond willow. After putting water on to heat, he moved a log stool over fairly close to me and started peeling the wood.

"Sure are funny shaped pieces," I said.

"Yup, been eyein' 'em fer a long time. Couldn't figger out what I could do with 'em before," Sven said, holding one piece out away from himself. The willow was about four feet long and branched out into two pieces near the middle, forming a Y shape but with the pieces not very far apart.

"What are you going to do with them?" I asked. The old man just scrunched his shoulders and didn't say anything. He started his tuneless humming and I took that as a signal not to ask any more questions.

I studied Sven's face and tried to picture what he'd looked like in his younger days before bushy brows and beard took over his face like so much pucker brush. Small nose, I thought. Almost looks out of place. Got that turned-up end—just like mine. I tried looking at my own nose, crossing my eyes and opening my mouth in the process. Sven glanced at me and his face turned into an amused frown.

"Whatcha makin' faces fer, son?" he asked.

I was embarrassed but decided to answer truthfully. "I was just thinking how our noses are shaped alike. We've both got that little knob on the end. Got mine from my mom. She always threatened to go have her nose fixed by one of those plastic surgeons but Dad would always tell her he liked it the way it was and then he'd kiss her on the end of it."

Sven's amused frown vanished and the now familiar wide-eyed hurt look took over his face as he quickly put down the willow and knife and walked over to the stove. Sensing the change in mood, I hoped he wouldn't go off and leave me, but he just stoked the fire and busied himself cleaning up the breakfast dishes.

I turned and faced the wall and studied the knots scattered helter-skelter, the hardened pitch bubbles adding their own decoration, and the funny maze of small grooves meandering in all directions. Worms, Dad had explained, get in under the bark and make their little trails which show up when the logs are peeled. I dozed off and woke to find Sven back on his stool peeling the willow.

My mouth felt dry, and not wanting to disturb Sven, I asked, "May I get up and get a drink of water?"

"Nope, I'll git ya some."

"Guess I had quite a nap," I said as Sven handed me the drink. "You've got the thing nearly all peeled. Pretty piece."

"Yup—jest gotta do the diamonds now." I watched as he worked the dry areas where the "diamonds" had to be cut out with a knife. Sven looked at me and asked if I wanted to work on a piece.

Thought you'd never ask," I said and positioned myself so that my hands were free. Sven handed me a round piece of wood about ten inches long. "My knife's in my pants pocket," I continued. "I'll try to handle it better than I did your axe." Sven grinned.

Turning the piece around in my hands, I remarked that it didn't have any diamonds in it. "Never mind about that," Sven said. "Jest peel it careful-like so's there won't be no nicks in it." We worked on in silence. And although the day dragged on as if set in slow motion, I felt welcome and at home here with Sven.

His greeting to me the next morning was a pleasant surprise. I woke to find him standing near my bunk.

I blinked a couple times trying to get my bearings and to make sure that, yes, it was Sven grinning broadly and holding a pair of diamond willow crutches in his hands. "Here, try these on fer size," he said.

Swinging my legs out over the side, I took one of the crutches Sven handed me. I recognized the piece where my hand went as the piece I'd worked on. Soft white fur cushioned the part that fit under the arm. Sven handed me the other one. Using the new crutches for support, I stood on my good foot, swung back and forth a bit to get used to being upright again, and then circled the cabin floor, ending back at my bed. "They work great!" I said. "And they're just the right size. How did you get them so perfect?"

"Measured ya while ya slept," Sven chuckled, looking as pleased and excited as I felt.

"Wait till Dad sees these—he'll want a pair just like 'em. Hope he doesn't need a pair, though." For a moment it seemed that thoughts of my dad would crowd out the happy feeling of being able to be up and around again, and it seemed as if Sven read my mind when he said, "Don't worry about yer pa. He kin take care of hisself. Long hike up there. Usta make a trip there myself ever' year or so but not anymore. Went sheep huntin'—needed meat. That's sheep hide on yer crutches."

"Soft," I murmured as I halfway petted the padding and tried to connect the picture I had in my mind of a beautiful white animal standing majestically on a cliff that looked like a fortress—and the need of an old man for meat or a boy for cushioning on a pair of crutches. I put them down and started to get dressed.

"Whoa there a minute, son," Sven said. "Jest cuz

ya got new pegs don't mean ya kin be up all day yit."
He gently cupped his hands under my heel and told me
to swivel my foot around. I winced. "Tell ya what," he
continued. "Ya kin git up today to eat and we'll see how
things are tomorrow. Good deal?"

"Good deal," I sighed, realizing that I didn't have
much choice in the matter. The choosing came a couple days later, however, when Sven announced that since
I was doing so well on the crutches, we could go fishing, that is if I wanted to. We spent the morning fixing
up what Sven called his "super-duper grayling gitters."
I watched as he tied delicate-looking fishing flies using
fine sinew, caribou hair and an assortment of feathers.
He worked silently for the most part but every once in
a while would explain about the materials he was using.
The sinew was from caribou leg and he liked to use the
caribou hair because it was hollow and would float well.
Each time he used a feather he'd tell me if it was from
a ptarmigan or duck. I marveled at how Sven's gnarled
fingers could produce such delicate work.

"Want to try one?" he finally asked. "Hard on the old
eyes."

"Hard on the old fingers, too," I said later as I held
up a rather flamboyant creation for Sven to see.

"Looks like we oughta swat that one," he teased.

"Or spray it with something," I laughed.

"Perty good fer the first one. Keep at it. Them grayling ain't very fussy."

And Sven's prediction proved right when we arrived
at the fish hole downstream from the cabin in the early
afternoon. I could hardly wait to get my line in the water.
Sven fixed me a place on shore where I could sit on a log

but still reach the water. I had my own fish pole. Sven stepped back away from the pool and returned with a makeshift pole he'd stashed away in the bushes.

"Usually keep a riggin' at my fishin' holes—jest have to carry my flies," he remarked as he went about tying on one of his special creations. "Git ready fer a watery explosion!"

And that's what it seemed like—no nibble, no gentle pulling, no hint that something might be interested in the bait. The strike was quick, sure, splashy and exciting. I found it a bit awkward trying to reel in while sitting, and after finally hooking into a lunker, stood firmly on both feet, forgetting about the sore foot. It buckled under me. I lost my balance and fell headfirst into the pool. Sven came in after me. Moments later, we sat on the shore, dripping wet and shivering, and the sound of an old man's laughter rippled through the alders, and on through the nearby spruces while he sputtered out the words, "Didn't mean that kinda watery explosion!"

19

"Yer gittin' real cagey with them pegs, Jeff," Sven remarked as he plunked an armful of wood down by the barrel stove.

"Yup, probably won't need 'em much longer. Guess that bath in the creek the other day helped my foot. Doesn't seem near as sore this morning. Okay to start walking on it?"

"Give it a try but take it easy first off." It seemed good to be rid of the bulky bandage which Sven had removed the night before, replacing it with a smaller one.

"Bet you'll be glad to get your mukluk back," I said, trying to see if I could get my foot into my own boot. Sven had gone out to his cache the day we'd gone fishing and brought in a well-worn but soft mukluk for me to wear over the bum foot.

"Maggie's mother made these fer me years ago—ain't worn 'em fer a while," he'd explained. The top of the mukluk had about a two-inch band of pretty beadwork trimming it. The caribou leg part of the mukluk was in fairly good shape but the home-tanned moose hide sole had several holes worn through. "Always intended to get 'er to put new bottoms on 'em but now she don't see too good no more," Sven said.

"Looks like I'll need more than new bottoms for this boot," I said, struggling to ease my foot into my cut shoe. "I think I could get it on better if the cut was just a little bigger—gonna need a new pair anyway."

Sven took out his knife and made an extra slit on each end of the slash in the boot.

"Yippie!" I yelled as I got the shoe on and stood on both feet for the first time in several days. "Looks like I'm back in business." Sven seemed to share my joy although he kept reminding me all morning to take it easy and slow down and not be so frisky. And by the time we'd eaten our lunch, I was ready to follow his advice. I took the shoe off and reached for my crutches. Sven squinted at me with a look that said maybe I should've paid more attention to what he'd been telling me.

"I know, I know," I commented. "Think I'm getting a case of cabin fever—need to be doing something."

"Tell ya what," Sven said. "You stay here 'n rest yer foot this afternoon while I go up the creek and do some diggin'. Tomorrow we'll go do a bit of gold pannin'."

"How far?" I asked.

"Less'n a mile. Ya kin take yer crutches along tomorrow just in case ya need 'em." I nodded but fully intended to try to wing it on my own. Sven left after picking up his rifle and saying he'd be back by supper time, and maybe with a fresh rabbit or grouse.

Deciding to lie down and rest my foot for a while, I looked around the cabin for something to read. Noticing an old book on one of the shelves, I reached for it and decided that it must be the book of English poems which Sven had mentioned back there on the trail the day we'd been down at the lake looking at the swans. I remembered that he'd quoted something about swans singing before they died but I couldn't remember who he said had written it. Knowing that it would be like looking for a needle in a haystack, I nevertheless decided to thumb through the book and see if I could find the quotation, thinking all the time how proud my teacher would be of me but that I'd better not tell my friends back home that I'd spent time in the wilds of Alaska with an old English literature book!

I shouldn't have worried, though, because I didn't get very far in the book before a drowsiness wrapped itself around me and I fell asleep and dreamed about swans swimming around in circles and occasionally putting their heads way back and singing a mournful song before flying off into the distance. Dozing fitfully, I woke up when the book dropped out of my hands and onto the floor.

Not knowing how long I'd slept nor wanting Sven to come home and find me in bed, I decided to get up and move around. When I reached to get the book up off the floor, I noticed that an old picture had fallen out of it. Picking it up, I glanced at it briefly and started to tuck it back into the book. Then I decided to take a closer look. Brown and crinkled around the edges as if it'd been handled many times, the picture was a snapshot of a man and woman standing under a sprawling tree with a swing hanging awkwardly on one of the branches. I stared at the picture for a long time. It seemed that there was just something familiar about it but then I'd seen lots of pictures of people standing under trees. I put the book with the picture inside back on the shelf and headed outside the cabin.

I suddenly realized that rippling water wasn't the only thing I was hearing. Off in the distance, low, rhythmic calls added their voice to the northland woods and seemed to be getting closer. Sounds like an owl, I thought, as the five staccato notes kept getting louder and louder. And when a giant bird swooped in and perched itself in one of the tall spruce trees not too far from the cache, I recognized it as a Great Horned Owl by its size and the tufts on its ears. I'd never seen an owl this big before except in a picture. Sitting as still as I could so as not to disturb it, I watched as it scanned the ground, jerking its head first one way and then another. Once in a while every top part of its light-colored breast would go in and out as it pumped out its hoots—Who-Who-Who-oo-Whoo-Whoo, Who-Who-oo-Whoo-Whoo. Off in the distance a faint echo answered and it too seemed to be getting closer and closer.

Just when I was beginning to think that maybe we'd be having an owl convention, I saw Sven shuffling down the trail. It didn't take long to realize that he was the echo and he sounded as owlish as Mr. Owl himself. "I always talk back to the owls," he whispered as he plunked himself down beside me. "They think I'm one of 'em. You answer 'im next time he hollers." We sat there quietly but didn't have long to wait. The owl puffed out another string of who-whos and I answered as best I could. Looking somewhat baffled, the big creature flapped his wings and took off upstream. We watched him disappear but continued to sit still until a final distant call let us know he probably wouldn't be back for a while.

"That was sure neat, seeing that owl and watching while he hooted," I said. Sven nodded. "How did the mining go?" I continued.

"Did a bit of diggin' but ran outa steam. Sure is aggravatin' not to be able to carry on like I usta." I could understand his frustration after being laid up a few days with the ailing foot. But I knew it was going to get better. I wondered if things would ever get better with Sven.

"Can we still go try tomorrow like you said?"

"Sure, we'll give 'er a try."

Sven kept his promise and mid-morning found us upstream at a spot which had been fairly shallow but that Sven had dug out until there was a deeper middle part where he'd removed the loose gravel and rocks. He explained that we had to get down to bedrock because that's where the gold would be if there was any there. He filled a gold pan with clay-like dirt and showed me how to keep swishing it around and washing off the top layers until there was just some fine stuff left in the bottom. It took a while for me to get the hang of it and I kept watching for big nuggets but didn't find any.

Working with the shovel a short way upstream from where I was panning, Sven called out, "Found anything?"

"No," I answered. "Think the grayling swallowed them all."

"Let me give it a try," Sven said and I limped up and handed him the pan. "Oughta be something in here." I watched as he skillfully worked the pan back and forth, occasionally dipping it at an angle into the water with no apparent break in his rhythm. He moved it lots faster than I did and when he got it down until there was hardly anything left in the pan, he handed it to me again.

"See them dull yellow specks clinging' to the side down there at the bottom? That's gold."

"It is? Need a magnifying glass to see it," I said. "I thought we might find some big nuggets."

"Well, there's always the chance we might but this's

better'n nuthin'.'" Sven took a small vial out of his pocket and went about retrieving the few tiny pieces from the gold pan. As he did so he blurted out, "Gold! Gold! Gold! Gold! Bright and yellow, hard and cold."

"Sounds real poetic, Sven," I said. "You just make that up?"

"Nope. Some old English poet named Thomas writ that." He held up the vial with the few flecks in it.

They don't look very bright to me and they're almost too dull to be yellow," I commented.

"Maybe that guy Thomas polished his." Sven grinned.

"By the way," I continued, "Yesterday I read some in your old book of English poems—I was trying to find that quote about the swans singing before they die. Couldn't find it, though." I filled up the pan with dirt again and swished with added vigor, fueled by the hope that maybe I'd find something now that I knew what to look for. I didn't get anything in the first pan but ended up with a few flecks in the second one.

"Eureka!" I yelled, "I got some," and turned around to ask Sven for the vial. He was nowhere in sight. Just as I started to call out his name, I caught a glimpse of him hustling down the trail in the direction of the cabin.

20

Puzzled by Sven's leaving in such a rush and not even telling me he was going somewhere, I decided to call it quits on the panning and go after him. I wanted to keep the precious gold I'd panned, so I got each of the four small flecks to stick to my finger and then flicked them into my shirt pocket. Probably never find them again, I thought, but I was determined to keep them. I was glad I'd followed Sven's advice and brought the crutches with me because it made the going faster than trying to hobble along mostly on one foot.

Worn out by the time I got back to the cabin, I was glad to see smoke coming out the chimney because it meant that Sven would probably be fixing us something to eat. As I walked by the end of the building I heard Sven's voice. Probably trying to explain to himself why he left me back there at the creek, I thought somewhat bitterly, but when I heard a familiar second voice, I knew he wasn't talking to himself. It was a good thing the cabin door was open because I think I would've gone right through it.

"Dad," I squealed.

"Hi, Jeff boy, how're you doing?" We hobbled toward each other and before I knew it, Dad was rubbing his prickly whiskers all over my face and giving me a bear hug that any grizzly would've been proud of. Then we both stood back and pointed to each other's foot, each mouthing the same question, "How's...?"

"Mine's doing great," I said. "Still a bit sore—and look at the diamond willow crutches Sven made for me." I picked them up and handed them to Dad.

"I may have to borrow them for a while," Dad commented as he eased himself down on a stool. "Guess the hike up in the hills was a bit more than I bargained for."

"How did things go?" I asked. "We really didn't expect you back for a couple more days at least." Dad reached for the cup of hot tea Sven handed him and took a couple sips before answering. I could tell by the way he raised his left eyebrow and stared at the floor that perhaps things hadn't gone as well as he'd planned.

He let out a long breath and said, "Well—sure is good tea, Sven."

"Well—what, Dad?" I interrupted.

"Well, first of all, it took me an extra day to get there because of my foot," Dad explained. "And when I did get there, I found that a landslide had come down and buried the whole thing."

"Well, I'll be..." Sven blurted out.

"What a bummer!" I exclaimed. "First the beavers and now this." It was my turn to shake my head and wonder. "So what did you do?"

"Stayed around for a day, made some notes and sketches. And guess what? I found the most beautiful little flowers growing up there—alpine azaleas and arctic bell heather, tiny little things. I pressed some to take to your mom and took lots of pictures." Dad's enthusiasm returned as he talked about the flowers and told about seeing some Dall sheep lambs playing around the craggy hillsides. "Wish you'd been with me, Jeff," he said. "But looks like you made out fine here."

"Sure did. Sven wouldn't let me do anything at first, but we did get to go fishing and today we went gold panning."

"Did you find any?"

"Sure did, got some right here in my pocket," I answered. "Sven, could I have the vial you had at the creek? I'd like to put my gold in it." Sven handed it to me with what I thought was a slightly embarrassed look and stood there watching as I took my shirt off and tried to retrieve the tiny nuggets.

"Prub-ly got lost in yer pocket fuzz-boos," he finally chuckled.

"Yeah, probably—in the fuzz-boos," I laughed. "Haven't heard that expression for a long time. Grandma Olsen always said I had more fuzz-boos in my pockets than anyone she'd ever seen. She always took my clothes outdoors and shook out all the pockets before washing 'em. Well, here's one nugget, anyway—see, Dad?"

"Better get out my magnifying glass," Dad teased. I found the other three pieces of gold and put them in the small container.

Holding the vial up to more closely examine the tiny flecks huddled together in the bottom, I said, "Eureka, we're rich!" Turning around so I could show our haul to Sven, I noticed that he'd moved over to his bed where he sat hunched over, clutching his chest and gasping for breath.

Dad moved quickly over to Sven and got him into his bed and lying down. He checked his pulse and spoke quietly to him and told him he was going to be okay. He looked up at me and mouthed the words, "He's okay."

Sven finally quit moaning and his breathing seemed more regular. "Old ticker actin' up agin'," he murmured and then dozed off. Dad stayed by his bedside for a while and then busied himself getting us something to eat. He seemed to be limping more than he had before and when he said we'd stick around Sven's place for a few days, I nodded my head in agreement.

We talked in hushed tones as we ate and Dad kept checking Sven's breathing. "What do you suppose brought that on?" I asked.

"Oh, it's hard to tell. How was he earlier today?" Dad asked. "Did he seem to be feeling okay?"

"Seemed full of energy and enthusiasm when we went out gold panning," I said, "but he did pull one of his Sven's out at the creek. He left me there without telling me he was coming back to the cabin."

"Hmm, that's strange. Can you remember what you'd been talking about right before he left?"

"Well, let's see. He'd quoted something about gold that was written by an old English poet and I told him I'd read some in his book on English poems the day before when he'd been gone for a while. That's all I can remember. I kept on panning and when I finally found something, I turned around to show him and he was gone." Dad looked puzzled, too, and checked on Sven again. He seemed to be sleeping peacefully.

"By the way, Dad, there was an old picture in the poetry book. Two people standing under a tree. I've been thinking about it off and on all day. Something about it looked familiar but I can't quite decide what it was."

"Well, let's take a look," Dad said and he tiptoed to the shelf and got the book. Pushing his plate aside, he sat at the table and thumbed through the book looking for the picture. "Don't see any picture in here," he said and handed it to me. I couldn't find it either. I walked over to the shelf to see if it had fallen out and looked on the floor but there was no picture anywhere.

"That's funny," I said. "I know the picture was there when I put the book back yesterday. Another case of a missing picture," I said as spookily as I could.

"And speaking of a missing picture," Dad said, "I found our family picture in my pack. Must be getting forgetful in my old age."

21

"Think we could strike out for home tomorrow, Jeff?" Dad asked after taking a good look at my foot. I'd been bandage-free for two days, there was no more swelling, and other than a slight tingle now and then, my foot felt fine. Dad seemed much more rested than when he first got back from the trek to the hills, and Sven was clearly on the mend. He'd laid low for a couple days after the fainting spell and his face looked a bit gaunt but he was in good humor.

"Sure, I'm game," I commented. "Sven will probably be glad to get us out of his hair."

"Yeah, think we've just about worn out our welcome," Dad chuckled. "Sven isn't used to having folks move in on him like this, are you, Sven?" The old man cleared his throat and seemed embarrassed at the question.

"I'll miss ya's both," was all he said. And I knew I'd miss him, too. Even with his unpredictable moods, there was something about Sven that made me feel comfortable when I was around him. I liked the way he felt about the animals, and how he liked to fish, and carve wood and accept the Alaskan wilderness on its own terms. And when we were all packed up the next day and ready to leave, I felt a lump in my throat as big as if I'd tried to swallow a gum ball.

"Hope ya don't need them crutches before ya git home," Sven said, half teasing. I'd strapped them to my pack, not because I thought I'd need them, but because Sven had made them, they were mine and a special souvenir of a special time. "I'll try to come see ya's before ya leave—gotta see them swans, anyway," Sven continued.

And the swans were much on our mind as we approached Copper Lake two days later. We'd taken our time on the return trip and Dad had scouted out another area where he wanted to check caribou browse and ground cover.

"Think you might set up a different study plot, Dad?" I'd asked.

"It's a bit late for that now—unless I plan to come back for a few more summers. You know, this was supposed to be my last year here." Dad didn't even try to hide his disappointment. There was no disappointment waiting at the pond, however, and we spent our lunchtime marveling at the changes in the three babies that really didn't look like babies anymore.

"Look how big they're getting," I remarked as we watched them glide along in and out among the weeds, occasionally almost disappearing as they fed underwater. "They should be big enough to fly pretty soon, shouldn't they?" I asked.

"No, they don't fly until they're about 13 to 15 weeks old," Dad replied. "But they'll be fully feathered before that."

"The mother must get impatient with 'em—it's a wonder she just doesn't take off," I said.

"Oh, no, she wouldn't leave them. Actually, she won't be able to fly either after a while. The adults molt every season—and the ones with young molt later than non-breeding swans. She probably won't be able to lead her young ones out of here until sometime in early September."

"Well, I guess we won't be here to see them go, will we?"

"No, by then we should be back home with Mom and Sis and you'll be back in school."

"Don't spoil the day by reminding me," I said. I hadn't been thinking too much about home because every time I did, I thought about Tippy and that she wouldn't be there when I got back. Dad had said we could get another dog but I knew we would never have another one like Tip.

"Well, speaking of home, our Alaskan home, that is," Dad said, picking up his load, "we'll never get there if we don't start trotting."

"Yeah, man," I replied, "we both look like we're hot to trot. Saw you limping a while ago—yah, yah."

"Needn't rub it in—but we do make a good pair. At least we can sympathize with one another." But the challenge called for more than sympathy. Dogged determination egged us on and we were one worn-out pair when we finally rounded the end of Tanada Lake and inched our way up the trail to the cabin. To our surprise, the door was open and a grinning Joe Nilchik greeted us. Jimmy stood rather shyly behind him but when Dad and Joe both started talking at the same time, we joined in. It was a happy reunion.

Joe explained that he'd come with Jimmy the day before and that they'd stayed all night in the cabin hoping we'd be back. Jimmy could stay for a few days just as he'd promised us.

"I was very disappointed when you weren't here,"

Jimmy said, "but my Dad kept saying you might come."

"Well—I'm glad you waited for us," I said. "Didn't know for a while if we'd make it or not." We spent the evening getting caught up on all the news and explaining our longer-than-planned visit with Sven. Joe said he'd made a trip back to his village and that everyone was talking about a big government project that might be built in the area—some kind of airplane detecting system. Said that they were going to do a bunch of wildlife studies first.

"You be good man for that, Larry," he said to Dad.

"I'd have to be more successful than what I've been here lately," Dad replied. "But it does sound interesting—just might check it out when I get a chance."

Joe left early the next morning after telling Jimmy to help us out and that he would come back after him in about a week. "Good, now I'll have two helpers," Dad commented. "I'll think up lots for them to do."

And that he did. We spent a few days getting rested up and putting things in order. Jimmy was a good helper and didn't complain when we had to pack water and do laundry. We had time for fun, too. He'd brought his baseball mitt with him and we spent lots of time playing catch each day after the chores were done. He had a good arm and when I complimented him on it, he looked shy and commented that he'd really wanted to play little league this year but couldn't because his dad wanted him at fish camp.

"Maybe next year," I said.

"Maybe," Jimmy answered but not very convincingly. "My dad said I might have to be big man at fish camp next summer. He might go to work on that big project."

"I'll come up and help you," I kidded. "I'd have to do better than what I've done this summer, though. Talk about your first class goofer-upper. I think if Dad ever comes back here, he'll probably leave me home and bring my sister. This was supposed to be his last summer here, you know."

I thought about that a lot as Jimmy and I went for short hikes around the place. I was beginning to feel more and more at home here in the wilderness of Alaska. There was just something about this land that seemed to crawl down inside you when you weren't looking, and once it was there, it became part of your being. There was so much life around even if it didn't look like it at times. And surprises—the country was full of surprises—some good, some bad.

Dad kept warning us about bear surprises as Jimmy and I meandered further away each day. We already knew about moose surprises. But on one particular afternoon it was a trio of caribou which surprised us as we topped a bushy knoll and scanned down the other side. They didn't seem to know we were there and we settled ourselves down to watch them browse on the low growth.

"Pretty good shot," Jimmy whispered. "I could really pick off that big one right from here." He lifted his arms into an aiming position and made believe shooting at the caribou in the lead. "Pshh—pshh! *Udzih* dead."

"*Udzih*?" I repeated after him.

"Yeah, *Udzih*. Means caribou."

"But why would you want it dead?" I asked. Jimmy didn't answer but looked at me with a puzzled expression on his face. He shook his dark head and a sudden shadow seemed to come down over his usually-laughing eyes.

He muttered something under his breath and didn't say much for the rest of the afternoon.

Later that evening when I had a minute alone with my dad, I told him about what had happened. "Jimmy may have thought you were criticizing him for wanting to shoot the caribou," Dad explained. "He looked at the animal as something of value to his family. It represents food for the table and hide for boots and mittens. It doesn't mean he doesn't have respect for the animal—he just looks at it differently." I tried to understand.

And it was Jimmy's turn to try to understand when I asked him if he wanted to go fishing for grayling the next day. "You got fish trap?" he asked.

"No," I replied, "just fish poles."

"Slow way. Just get one at a time with that kind."

"But all we want is one at a time, isn't it?" I asked. Jimmy shrugged his shoulders. Dad gave us permission to go down to the stream at the head of the lake. I soon discovered that Jimmy had never fished with a fish pole before. He watched as I cast out the fly and had soon reeled in three flopping grayling. After hitting them a good thud on the head, I strung them on a forked stick and let them dangle in the water. I handed him the pole and said, "Your turn." He didn't seem very enthusiastic but took the pole and gave it a try. He missed the first couple strikes but soon landed a 15-incher and then gave the pole back to me.

Deciding that the four fish we had was all we need-ed to eat, I released the next two fish after taking them off the hook as gently as I could. I felt a little twinge of guilt because I knew Dad didn't want me to do that but I wasn't quite ready to call it quits when the fish were biting so good. Jimmy sat on the bank and watched, chewing on a piece of willow he'd peeled the bark off.

"How come you threw those fish back?" he asked. "They're just as big as the others."

"Those four are enough," I answered. "I really don't like them much anyway—too many bones." Jimmy looked puzzled.

"Why you keep on fishing then?"

"Well," I said, and I had to think about that for a moment. "I just like to fish. I like to feel them bite and try to pull away. I feel bad when I lose one. It's exciting reeling them in and seeing how big they are. I guess I just like to fish," I repeated. Somehow, I knew I wasn't doing a very good job explaining and when I tried to hand the rod back to Jimmy, he pushed it away with his hand, got up and walked slowly along the shoreline.

I felt awkward and decided to call it quits on the fishing and followed after Jimmy. Pointing to the mound where the now-abandoned swan's nest was, I said, "That's where the swan nested. She moved her three babies to that other small lake—Copper Lake. You ever been there?"

"Couple times," Jimmy answered. "Went muskrat hunting with my dad. And I been by there in the winter when we took some stuff to Sven with the dog team."

"Wanna go look at them?" I asked.

"Your Daddy won't care?"

"I suppose I could go ask him," I said, looking back towards the cabin. "But he'd probably say it was okay. He's been real busy lately and might be glad to have us out of his way a little longer." I never would have gone to see the swans by myself but I felt secure having Jimmy along. We left the fish dangling in the water, parked the pole upright against a bush, and before long were on our way to visit the swans.

Fairly sure of the trail, I led the way after explaining that it couldn't be too far because three baby swans had waddled the distance along behind their mother not too long after they'd hatched. "You see them do that?" Jimmy asked.

"No, but they disappeared from the lake and then we saw them at Copper Lake."

"How do you know they're the same ones?"

"The mother has a real rusty neck. My dad says it's just a stain from where they feed in the winter. He said this female has a brighter stain than most—guess she must be a good eater. Maybe that's why she's so tough. Good thing, because she has to raise her young all by herself. Don't know why someone had to shoot the male." Jimmy didn't reply to that and I knew I shouldn't press the matter further.

We made pretty good time to the pond but couldn't see the swans anywhere. "Phooey!" I exclaimed. "Looks like we came on a wild goose chase."

"Thought we were looking for swans," Jimmy said.

"Well, we are," I replied.

"How come you said wild goose then?"

"Oh, never mind," I said after glancing at Jimmy and realizing he wasn't kidding. We struggled along the marshy edge of the pond to try to get a better view of the upper end. Jimmy led the way and hadn't gone too far when he held up his hand and motioned me to stop.

"There they are," he whispered.

"Think we can get closer?" I asked.

"We can try," Jimmy said, but finding the going just

too rough, he stopped and panned the shoreline on the other side. "Aha," he finally added, "follow me." We sloshed back down along the shore and were soon on the other side of the pond. Jimmy abruptly left the trail and ploughed through the brush on the right, acting as if he knew exactly where he was going. I had no choice but to follow. We hadn't gone far when he stopped, pushed back some bushes and pointed, grinning from ear to ear.

"See," was all he said. There nestled under some brush was a small homemade-looking canoe. Grabbing one end of it, Jimmy motioned for me to go around and pick up the other end. Lightweight yet fairly sturdy, the tiny canoe was nothing but painted canvas stretched over a crude wooden frame. "My dad's rat canoe," Jimmy explained with a note of triumph in his voice.

"Rat canoe?" I asked.

"Yeah, for hunting muskrats. You can carry it really easy from lake to lake. I wasn't sure just where it was because I didn't come last spring with my dad."

"Then how did you know where it was?"

Jimmy just grinned and said, "Indian sign." He pointed to a dead willow stuck in the ground with the root end up in the air. We easily carried the small craft to the water's edge and gently slipped it into the pond. We tested it for leaks and it seemed to be okay. Jimmy went back away from shore and reappeared with a paddle. "Only found one," he said. "Guess tsa' chewed up the other."

"Tsa'—let me guess—wolverine?"

"No."

"Porcupine."

"No."

"I give."

"Beaver," Jimmy said, as he climbed into the canoe and pulled a rather rotten-looking rope in behind him.

"I should have known," I said with a fake groan, "my dad's best friend." I climbed in after Jimmy, nearly capsizing the boat in the process.

"Careful," Jimmy warned. "This kind real tippy." After telling me to sit in the bottom, he knelt up front and started to paddle first on one side and then the other. We glided along slowly but smoothly, heading towards the upper end where the swans were. They continued feeding, seemingly unaware of the intruders spying on them. We stopped finally and snuggled up as close to the bank as we could, trying to settle in behind some brush reaching out over the water. With hardly a ripple to mar the glassy expanse, bright yellow lilies polka-dotted the surface, their beauty multiplied by the clear reflections. Skimming along gracefully, the four swans cast their spell over us here in the middle of the Alaskan wilds and I was glad that we'd come. Even the mosquitoes seemed to let up for a while as we basked in the warmth of the afternoon sun.

Wishing that Dad and Sven could've been here, too, I suddenly realized that we'd been gone from the cabin for quite a while and should head back. I leaned forward to whisper to Jimmy who had just started to point frantically in the direction of the swans. Although we hadn't made any disturbance, they were obviously upset about something. The mother flapped her wings, stretched out her neck and sounded an alarm which echoed up and down the pond. We soon saw the reason for her distress. Quickly bearing down on the young and ignoring the mother's threats, a large cat-like animal swam out from shore.

"Wow, a link,' Jimmy exclaimed, not even trying to be quiet anymore.

"A link? What's a link?"

"You know—like a bobcat."

"Oh, you mean a lynx?"

"Call it whatever you want but it looks like it's going to get one of them babies." We watched helplessly as it grabbed the young swan nearest to it and paddled back towards the shore with the mother in hot pursuit. Jimmy and I both started yelling, but if the lynx heard us, it chose to ignore the clamor. Soon reaching the shore, it stopped to shake itself for a moment, and then disappeared with the swan flopping around in its mouth. The mother herded her two young towards the other end of the pond.

"First time I ever see that," Jimmy said. "My dad told me about seeing a link getting ducks. Pretty brave to go after swans."

"I don't call it brave," I said. "I call it downright mean." I was stunned by what we'd seen and had a hard time mustering up any sympathy for the link or lynx or whatever it was. Jimmy muttered something about that the cat needed to eat, too, and didn't kill the swan just for the fun of it. And taking the paddle, he maneuvered the boat around while I tried to help by grabbing the bushes along the shore.

"Wish we had another paddle," I said. "Couldn't we find a pole or something that I could push with?" Jimmy said he'd go look for something, carefully got out of the boat and came back moments later with a rather skinny but sturdy pole.

"You have to be careful with that," he said as he climbed back in. "Get on your knees at that end and put the pole down close to the boat. Don't push too hard on it—just give a little shove when it touches bottom."

I soon got the hang of it and we moved along at a pretty good pace. Jimmy turned and gave me an approving glance and nodded his head in the direction of the shore and said, "Almost there." I could see the spot where we'd launched the canoe.

The water seemed to get deeper all of a sudden, however, and when I put the pole down the next time, I couldn't touch bottom. I reached out over the back end to make the pole go down further, and when I did, the boat lurched awkwardly and the next thing I knew we'd overturned and I was floundering around in the water. I started swimming towards the shore and looked around for Jimmy. Not seeing him anywhere, I panicked until I noticed that the canoe was slowly floating towards the shore and there was a thrashing in the water under it. Remembering that Jimmy had told me he'd never learned to swim, I angled towards the boat and yelled, "Keep kicking!"

When I got to shore, I realized we had another problem—the water stayed deep right up to the edge of the bank. Trying to stay afloat and figure out the best way to get out of the water, I didn't notice that we had company until a familiar voice called out, "Grab on, Jeff," and Sven reached down and got a firm grip on my outstretched arm. I reached around with my left and grabbed Jimmy just as he popped out from under the boat. Somehow the old man pulled us both up on the shore. He stood there eyeing us as we emptied out our boots and finally said, "Nice day fer a swim." Jimmy and I looked at each other sheepishly but didn't say anything. We all knew what a narrow escape we'd just had.

"Sven, you sure have a knack for knowing when you're needed," I said a short time later as we found an open sunny spot and tried to dry off.

"And you seem to have a knack fer fallin' in the water," was his reply.

"This is the second time you've had to pull me out. How'd you happen to come along when you did?"

"Well, bin sorta restless since you and yer dad left. Thought I'd come check on the swans. Seen you two from the end of the lake and jist headed up this way. Thought you might take a spill when I seen you with that pole. Them rat canoes ain't very stable."

"Yeah, I know—Jimmy warned me and just when I thought I was doing so great, ker-splash!"

"You done good," Jimmy said. "That pole I got was just too short." I gave him an appreciative glance and then looked back at Sven.

"Did you see what happened to one of the babies?" I asked.

"Knew there was some sort of ruckus goin' on but couldn't see that that good to tell what it was," Sven said.

"A lynx swam out and grabbed one of them and took off with it," I sputtered, looking down at the ground and busying myself with trying to squeeze the last bit of water out of my boots. When I did look up, Sven was staring at me with a pained expression that let me know he understood how I felt. He mumbled something about the law of the wild not always seeming fair but that we couldn't do much about it.

"How's yer dad?" he finally asked, obviously trying to change the subject. "I'm s'prised he let you two come out here all by yerselves."

"He didn't," I confessed. "He doesn't know we're here."

Sven's wide-eyed look seemed to spread over his face, and putting his hands on his hips, he almost shouted, "Ya's better hightail it home afore he comes lookin'!" But it was already too late. Dad came charging through the brush.

22

With documents spread all over the place, Dad spent the next week working inside and not talking very much. He seemed preoccupied and I'd felt almost alone at times after Jimmy left. So when we got up one morning and he asked me if I felt like hitting the trail again, I was all for it.

"I need to get something in the mail right away and since we don't have a carrier pigeon service out here, I thought we'd hike out to the Nabesna Road and hitch a ride to the Slana post office."

"How far is it to the road?" I asked.

"Only a couple miles as the crow flies but we'll have to skirt around some swampy areas and it's not the best walking in the world. Should be able to make it by noon if we leave early enough and don't have a run-in with a mama bear."

"Just don't let me carry your pack," I said.

"That episode seems like a long time ago, doesn't it?"

"Sure does—it's been a busy summer."

"Things are sort of winding down for us now, though, and we might be heading home soon—it all depends on what kind of a reply I get back on the stuff I'm sending in."

"What's this all about, Dad? We haven't had to bother with mail before?"

"Well, I've put together a packet of material for my advisors at the university. I'm making a proposal for some changes in my research. If they accept it, then we'll finish things up here in a jiffy and be on our way. If they don't accept it, well, I'm not sure what the next step will be. Losing two study plots this summer sort of threw a monkey wrench into my plans but... things will work out for us. They always do." Dad must have noticed the troubled look I got on my face because he rumpled up my hair and continued, "Cheer up, there, old buddy. We've had a good summer and I wouldn't change a thing—well, maybe a few things. But we've lots to be thankful for—the Good Lord's been watching over us."

"Yeah," I sighed. "Guess He hired Sven as a guardian angel. Still have a hard time to believe he was on hand to pull Jimmy and me out of the water. By the way, Dad, Jimmy never could understand why you didn't punish us for doing what we did. I told him I just thought you probably figured we'd been punished enough already."

"Right on, man, right on," Dad replied. "And guess what? We'll surprise Mom and Sis with a call while we're out there."

"Hope they don't have more bad news for us," I said, thinking of Tippy. But it was hard to stay moody for very long. Dad seemed more like his old self and I was excited at the thought of doing something different for a change.

And our hike wasn't that much different from all the others we'd taken through muskeg, brush and tundra. Long before reaching the highway, we could hear vehicles and see dust rising off in the distance. Finally crossing a small stream and noticing that the trail had widened considerably, we hurried along to the gravel road where I lifted my feet high and pounced down on the surface in sheer glee.

"Neato, what a boulevard!" I yelled.

"Say, you're acting a bit bushy, aren't you, boy?" Dad remarked but I noticed that he paraded back and forth, kicking a few stones along the way.

"Just call me Bushman of the North," I said, fluffing out my longer than usual hair and trying to make it look punky.

"Better tone it down a bit," Dad said. "I think I hear something coming." A pickup truck soon chugged into view and slowed down when the driver saw us by the side of the road.

"Where are you headed? Need a ride?" he asked. Dad explained that we were trying to get to the Slana post office. "You're welcome to hop up on the back. Front seat's kind of full," he continued. A dark-haired woman and several small children smiled shyly at us through the back window. "Just push some of that junk outa the way." We climbed in and made space for ourselves and our packs between oil barrels, gas cans, a chain saw, assorted ropes, chains and wire, and a huge set of caribou antlers.

The road was rough and dusty but it was better than walking the twenty odd miles to the post office. When we got there the driver got out of the truck, smoothed down his bushy black beard, reached out his hand and said, "Name's Gerald Littleton."

Dad shook his hand. "I'm Larry Nickerson and this is my son Jeff. We've been camping out at Tanada Lake all summer doing research on caribou browse. That's some rack you have there in the back of your truck—must be a record. You get it?"

"No," the driver replied, pushing back his well-worn visor cap and taking time to spit out a mouthful of tobacco juice. "I guided a fellow out of Chicago last fall. He was looking for a trophy but didn't think this was quite big enough so he left it here. Plans to come back in the fall and try again."

"You do any flying?" Dad asked.

"Yeah, some. Not much going on right now. Fly a few fishermen into Copper Lake now and again."

"Your plane on floats?"

"Yup."

"Any chance I could get you to fly something in to us at Tanada?"

"Sure," he said. Dad explained that he would be expecting some important mail in a couple weeks and needed someone to pick it up and bring it in. They went inside to talk to the postmistress and I strolled over to look at some horses in a corral nearby. I joined them when they came out of the small log building.

"We're staying in the little cabin on the north side of the lake," Dad explained.

"I know right where it is," Mr. Littleton said. "Trapped in there with my dad. We used to stay in the cabin once in a while."

"Ever find a wolverine in it?" I asked. He laughed when I went on to tell about how we were greeted in the spring.

"Do you ever see anything of that old prospector in there? Been there for years—sort of an odd old cuss."

"You mean Sven?" Dad asked.

"Yeah, that's his name—Sven Olsen. Met him years ago when I was just a kid. He used to stop in at our place once in a while but haven't seen him around for the past several years. Talked a blue streak whenever he came to visit but we never found out much about him—where he'd come from and all."

"Sounds like our Sven, all right. You say his last name is Olsen?"

"Think so. My dad used to call him that old Olsen hermit—guess he really wasn't that old, just looked old. Well, guess I'd better go along. Kids are restless. I've been promising them a trip to Glennallen for weeks. They like to go to that ice cream place. Don't get out very much—living way back in there." We said goodbye and went back into the post office after he drove off. The postmistress had told Dad we could use the phone to call Mom.

Dad talked first and then it was my turn. Guess I talked a mile a minute telling about the swans and Jimmy and Sven and that we'd just found out Sven's last name was Olsen. I started to tell her about the episode at Copper Lake but when Dad gave me the no-no look, I decided I'd better change the subject.

Mom said she missed us lots and would be glad when we got home. Then she asked to put Dad back on. Dad's voice seemed to get serious all of a sudden and he said such things as, "Well, I'm not sure," and "Don't get your hopes up," and "We'll work on it." After the call Dad chatted briefly again with the postmistress. She explained further about the Backscatter Radar project Joe Nilchik had mentioned. It was supposed to be a more reliable plane and missile detecting system but that some environmental studies would have to be completed before construction would begin. Dad seemed very interested and when the lady offered him a copy of a questionnaire which had been sent out to all the communities asking what skills and training folks had to offer, Dad took it and folded it carefully before stuffing it into his pocket.

"You don't happen to have a map showing the exact area where they plan to build this thing, do you?" Dad asked.

"No, but you could get one at the ranger station down the road a bit." I really didn't feel like walking and I was getting kind of hungry but Dad hustled us both over to the place. I looked around at the displays and listened in on the conversation. My ears really perked up when the ranger explained that some folks were worried about the effect of the planned project on migrating birds—and especially the Trumpeter Swans.

We spent some time looking at a large wall map and Dad pointed out where our cabin was and where Sven lived. When I asked Dad why there were stars at both places, the ranger must have heard me because he came over and explained that they'd put stars on to show the location of all the cabins inside the park and preserve areas.

"You ever see anything of that old duffer in there— name's Sven something or other?" the ranger asked.

"You mean Sven Olsen?" I blurted out and didn't even wait for an answer. "Sure have—he pulled me and Jimmy Nilchik out of Copper Lake not too long ago." I went on to explain what had happened.

"We've been trying to get in touch with him," the ranger continued. "Need him to sign a use permit for his cabin inside the preserve area. A couple of our guys were in there a few years back when all this land was set aside. Guess he didn't quite understand and thought we were trying to kick him out. He got very mad and run them off. No one seems to see him out here anymore. I would appreciate it if you could take the form in and get him to sign it if you happen to see him again."

"I'll give it a try," Dad said—rather reluctantly, I thought. "Sven sort of lives by his own code and we try to respect that as much as we can." The ranger stepped over to a file cabinet, took out a form, put it in an envelope, and wrote Sven's name on it.

"You guys on foot?" he asked as he handed Dad the envelope. Dad nodded and explained that we'd walked out to the highway and had hitched a ride to the post office. Reaching for his jacket, the ranger said, "I'm going to take a run back up to the lodge. You can ride along with me if you want." Soon sitting at the small lunch counter gobbling down hamburgers and fries, my dad and I kept smiling at each other as if we just couldn't believe our good fortune. The steady hum of the light plant out back somewhere vibrated throughout the room and had a sort of lulling effect on me, though, and after we ate I felt like having a nap. I think Dad felt the same way because he suggested that we set up camp at a spot not too far from the lodge.

"Great idea," I said. "Then we can come back for another burger soon as this one settles down." But it wasn't to be because some tourists came along and gave us a ride back to where we'd hit the main road earlier in the day. We rested by the little stream we'd crossed hours earlier and I guess we both had the same idea because when Dad even hinted that perhaps we should head home right away, I grabbed my pack and splashed across to the other side.

Dad set a much slower pace on the return trip and we didn't chat much except for when we stopped for a break. I kept thinking about Sven and was full of all sorts of questions. "Why do you suppose he never told us his last name was Olsen?" was the one I asked over and over again. "He knew my middle name was Olsen because I told him once. And I've mentioned Grandma Olsen several times," I explained to Dad. "In fact, the more I think about it, it seems that every time the name Olsen was mentioned, Sven took off for never-never land."

"You know, you just might be on the right track," Dad remarked. "But we'd better not try to read too much into all of this. I guess if Sven had wanted us to know that his last name was Olsen, he would have told us."

"You know what?" I think the next time I see him I'm going to say, 'Hi, Mr. Olsen.'" Dad gave me one of his looks and I added, "I jokes."

"I jokes?" Dad asked.

"That's what Jimmy says when he's teasing. By the way, if we leave earlier than planned, will I be seeing Jimmy again?"

"Joe said they'd be finishing up at fish camp fairly soon and asked us to give him a call from Gulkana airport on our way out. Said he and Jimmy would come see us off."

"Wish Jimmy could come visit us in Seattle sometime," I commented.

"Who knows, maybe he can," Dad replied.

"Jimmy asked me if I could come back sometime in the winter when he was training for the dog races."

"At least the lakes would all be frozen over then so we wouldn't have to worry about you guys almost drowning again," Dad teased.

"Then you think there's a chance I could come back

sometime?" I didn't even try to hide my excitement.

"Well, hard to say right now. I may be coming back myself, Lord willing, and this Backscatter project works out." I had lots to think about the rest of the way home as we tromped on in silence.

23

"Littleton ought to be flying in here any day now," Dad said early one evening. "Don't know where the past two weeks have gone." Dad had seemed much more relaxed after we got back from the trip to Slana. It was as if he'd finally decided he'd done all he could and was going to enjoy the rest of the time out here in the wilds. He still kept on doing some sketches and he made me get caught up with writing my observations about the swans, but we went fishing often, took an overnight trip to the beaver dam, checked a couple times on the swan and her two remaining young. Each day brought something new and I sort of sensed that Dad was trying to soak up every bit of whatever there was about this country that made it so special.

"But what if he comes in and then you decide to leave right away," I worried. "I don't want to go without saying goodbye to Sven. And you have to get him to sign that paper."

"Yeah, I know," Dad sighed, as if he didn't really relish the task. "He just might still show up in the next day or so. Said he'd see us before we left."

"Maybe pulling me and Jimmy out of the pond was too much for him."

"Nah, he's a tough old guy." And we were soon to find out just how tough he really was.

About noon the next day we heard a plane coming

and instead of just flying over as most of them did, it circled the lake, landed and then taxied over to where we'd hustled down to meet it. Gerald Littleton got out and handed Dad the piece of mail he'd been expecting. He had a concerned look on his face. "Say, I took a roundabout way in here today and flew over what I thought was that old Sven's place. Does he still live in that big cabin on Mineral Creek?" he asked.

Dad nodded. "Something wrong?"

"Well, looked like someone was lying out there in the yard by the cache. I swung back around a couple times to try to get a better look but he didn't wave or nothing."

"What's the closest place you could land around there?" Dad asked.

"There's that little pond just east of his place—it'd be about a mile or so to walk. Sort of hard to get in there this time of year because of all the lily pads but we could give it a try." Hurrying back to the cabin, Dad packed up some things and we were soon in the air heading for Sven's place. I looked down when we flew over Copper Lake and could see the swans and the place where Jimmy and I had taken the spill. Maybe saving our lives really had been too hard on Sven. Worry and guilt swirled around in my mind, muddying my thoughts and distracting from the excitement of seeing this part of the country from the air.

It wasn't long before the pilot swooped down lower and I heard him tell Dad that we'd fly in over the cabin to take a look. My stomach did a flip-flop as he banked the plane but I tried to ignore it and help look for Sven. We spotted him about halfway between the cache and the cabin. "Well, he isn't dead, anyway," the pilot called out over the roar of the engine. "He's moved from where he was before." We started climbing again and it wasn't long before we'd set down on the isolated pond.

"Great landing," Dad remarked.

"Thought those lily pads were going to grab us there once," Gerald said. "Want me to hike in there with you?"

"Well, that would be very helpful," Dad answered. "Apparently Sven is able to move but at this point we don't know how bad off he is." The hike to Sven's cabin seemed to take forever and I wondered how Dad knew where to go. There were well-worn game trails all through this country with no apparent main path. Dad kept looking at his compass and explained he'd plotted the route from the air.

Arriving at Sven's place a short time later, we found him lying face down and unconscious just outside his doorway. "Glad you're with us, Gerald. We'd have a hard time getting him inside. Besides that, it's starting to rain." Dad stepped inside and got a blanket to spread over Sven who groaned but didn't open his eyes. "Looks like the problem might be with his left leg," Dad continued. He and Gerald went looking for some splint material.

Sitting on the ground close to Sven, I had a hard time keeping the tears back but knew this was no time to cry. I kept telling Sven that we were there and he was going to be okay, that we would make him better, somehow knowing that I was really only trying to convince myself. Dad and Gerald came back with some make-do splints and fixed them on the outside of Sven's left leg. Making a makeshift stretcher out of some poles and the blanket, they gently carried him inside and placed him on a sleeping bag on the floor.

Dad sent me out to get some wood with the remark that he hoped we'd be as tough as Sven when we got old. He had dragged himself all the way over from the cache to the cabin door. I looked over to see if I could find any clues as to what had happened. The broken ladder flung haphazardly on the ground told the story and near it was an old wooden box whose contents were strewn all over the place. I took the wood in to Dad and told him I thought I should go up and pick the stuff up before it got wet. He agreed and said he'd get the fire going. I glanced down at Sven and didn't see any change.

The box had been full of old paper and magazines and I had most of the stuff picked up when a little brown folder crumbled in my hands and a bunch of pictures fell out. Scooping them up before they got wet, I noticed one of them was just like the picture I'd seen in Sven's old book but had disappeared that day we had gone gold panning. I carried all the stuff inside and set the box on the table.

"Dad," I said, "look. I think this is the picture I couldn't find that day when we were here before. And there's a whole bunch more here, too." Dad glanced down at the picture, frowned a bit, cocked his head to one side like he usually did when he was puzzled. He placed the picture back inside the folder and put them all back in the box.

"Those aren't ours," he said quietly.

Gerald kept checking on Sven and finally said, "I think we need to get help for the old guy. How about if I fly out and look into the possibility of getting a rescue helicopter in here? Don't think my plane should carry any passengers when trying to get off from the skinny place

we flew in on. You two could fly out with the rescue team
and they could drop you off at your cabin and then take
Sven on for medical help."

With a very thankful look, Dad kept nodding his
head in agreement. We were very thankful about an hour
later when we heard the plane flying over.

As evening approached, we took turns sitting on the
floor by Sven. "He's a very sick man," Dad whispered but
said we should keep up our chatter to him. I told him all
about the trip to Slana and what we'd been doing—that
we'd been to Copper Lake a couple times and that we'd
seen the three swans when we flew over today. Suddenly
I thought I detected a slight movement of Sven's eyes
and his mouth opened a bit but no sound came out. I
motioned for Dad to come and he wiped off Sven's face
with a damp cloth.

"Can you hear us, Sven?" Dad spoke slowly. "Jeff
here was telling you about seeing the swans today." The
old man moved his head slightly and mouthed something
and although sounds came out this time, we couldn't make
out what he was trying to say. "You just take it easy," Dad
said. "We're going to be right here with you." Sven continued to drift in and out of consciousness but each time
he came to, he seemed to stay awake a little longer. And
when he finally opened his eyes and looked up at us, Dad
said, "Welcome back, Sven, you've been out of it for a
while. Looks like you fell and hurt your leg." He seemed
to understand.

Still struggling to speak, he kept making the same
sounds over and over, and when I told Dad that I thought
he was trying to say something about a swan, Sven nodded his head slightly. "What about the swan?" I asked

rather loudly.

"On the shelf," came out in a raspy whisper.

"On the shelf?" I asked and Sven nodded again. Looking at Dad, I murmured, "I think he's delirious," but I did get up and go over to the shelf. Sitting next to the old English literature book was a beautiful hand-carved swan. I picked it up and carried it carefully over to Sven and knelt down beside him. "This swan—it's so beautiful—its neck looks so graceful. But it looks so familiar. Why do I have the feeling that I've seen it before?" I asked.

"It's almost an exact replica of the ones your mother has on her swan candleholders—except the wood's newer," Dad said quietly. We looked down at Sven and before drifting off again, he whispered, "Made those, too." Wide-eyed, Dad and I looked at each other. Dad checked his pulse and said, "Heartbeat's not very strong."

The next time Sven rallied, his speech seemed a little clearer and we could understand his mumbling—still something about the swan. "Do you mean the carved swan, Sven? I have it right here." Sven opened his eyes and then closed them again.

"Take-it-to-yer-Grand-ma-Ol-sen," he took a long time saying, "and-tell-her-I'm-sor-ry. Nev-er-quit-lov-in' Nellie, Nellie, Nellie." He repeated the name over and over until his voice trailed off and his labored breathing wound down like a train rumbling off in the distance.

Dad quickly checked his pulse again, and putting his arm around my shoulders, said softly, "He's gone." I sat there on the floor by Sven and didn't even try to control my sobs. I closed my eyes and let the tears squeeze themselves out and run down my face onto the blanket which

Dad had gently pulled up over Sven's face.

"He was my Grandpa, wasn't he," I finally blurted out.

"Yes," Dad answered.

"And I never even got to call him Grandpa once," I sobbed.

24

Two weeks later Dad and I stood on the muskegy edge of Copper Lake and watched as bush pilot Littleton swooped in low and spread Grandpa Olsen's ashes over the crystal clear water while three Trumpeter Swans swirled about, eventually sounding off their triumphant call as the plane hummed off into the distance. We bowed our heads and Dad prayed, thanking God for the time we'd been able to spend with Grandpa and for the special place he'd filled in our hearts.

It had been a difficult two weeks. The troopers had sent in a helicopter to get the body out and it had been taken into Anchorage for an autopsy and cremation. Dad made arrangements for his ashes to be returned to Gulkana where Gerald Littleton picked them up and flew them back to Tanada. We'd had to make another trip to Slana to call Mom and Grandma to tell them the news. They both agreed that Grandpa should stay here in the wilds that had been his home for so many years.

Dad and I spent a lot of time talking about Grandpa Olsen. My biggest question was how come no one had ever told me that I might have another grandfather somewhere?

"It was just something your ma's family never wanted to talk about," Dad explained. "Apparently your Grandma Nellie and Grandpa Sven ran off and got married without telling her folks. He was quite a bit older than she was and her folks didn't think he was good enough for her. They kept putting a lot of pressure on her to leave him, but about three months before your ma was born, he took off and no one ever heard from him again."

"Well, I can see now why he got so upset whenever her name was mentioned," I commented. "But when do you think he found out who we really were?"

"Oh, I think he first suspected long before you came to Tanada. He used to sit in my cabin and stare at the family picture I always had with me. I really think it was the picture of the candleholders on the mantle that clinched it in his mind, though. And then when you came with all your exuberance and tales of Grandma Olsen, well, I guess that settled it."

"And how about you, Dad? When did you get suspicious?"

"When we called your mother from Slana that day and you told her about Sven and that we'd just found out what his last name was, she got all excited and reminded me that her dad's name had been Sven. Then all those other things began to add up, but I didn't want to say much until I was sure. That old picture really settled it though as far as I was concerned. I'd seen the same picture in an old album your ma has. That was your grandparents by the old tree at the old home place where your grandma grew up."

"Now I remember why it looked so familiar. That was the old tree I used to swing on years ago before it blew down."

"Well, no matter what," Dad had remarked, "your Grandpa was proud of you and you brought joy into his meager life when he most needed it. And whether he was right or wrong for what he did—I guess it's not up to us to be the judge and jury."

"Well, all I can say is, I was glad he was out there by Copper Lake a few weeks back," I remarked.

"I agree," Dad replied. "Oh, how I agree. So, we'll just try to remember the happy times."

But it was thoughts of those happy times that brought about sadness when we packed up a few days later and prepared to leave our Tanada wilderness home. Dad's advisors had accepted his proposal for finishing his research project and arrangements had been made for Gerald Littleton to fly us out to Jack Lake along the Nabesna Road and then drive us to Gulkana Airport to get a flight to Anchorage.

As we lifted off Tanada Lake and watched it dwindle down to a puddle, I gave a long last look and knew in my heart that someday I'd be back. I'd left part of myself there to merge with the wild things that swam and ran and flew and lived and died, fairly or unfairly, but never without a struggle.

Joe and Jimmy met us at Gulkana. They'd heard about Grandpa but didn't know the full story until Dad explained why we'd done what we did with the remains. Dad and Joe stepped aside to chat and Dad suggested that Jimmy and I go for a stroll along the edge of the runway. Jimmy was wearing his beaded belt and knife with 'our' initials on the handle. After we'd gone a short distance he stopped, took the belt off and handed it to me. "My mom said to give it to you." Taking it and looking it all over, I finally placed it around my waist, at the same time I slipped my knife and sheath from the belt I was wearing.

"And if my mom was here, I know she'd want you to

have this." Jimmy looked surprised as I handed him my knife and sheath with the letters JON tooled into it. He examined it carefully and then put it in his jacket pocket. Dad called us to come back because the plane would be leaving soon. He and Joe were standing by Joe's truck and Dad motioned for us to come over.

"They brought you a surprise," Dad said. Jimmy opened the front door of the truck and took out a small cardboard box and handed it to me. Before I even got the top open I could tell there was something alive in it. Putting the box on the ground, I took out a dark, round, warm puppy with bright blue eyes, a perfect mask—and a little white tip on the end of its tail.

The End

ABOUT THE AUTHOR

Althea Hughes
Secret of the Swans

After moving from Maine to Alaska in 1953, Althea and Kenneth Hughes have spent 66 years settling in to the firm grip Alaska offers to those who accept the uniqueness, beauty, and special challenges of the North Country. After years of teaching, homesteading, raising a family, running a business, community involvement and a sort of retirement, Althea responded to the yen to write.

In the latter part of the 1980s, she got the urge to move on a bit from just writing nature articles—mostly about birds—and work on a juvenile fiction tale centered in Alaska. The result was entitled Secret of the Swans and in 1990 was submitted to two publishing companies who politely wrote that the story didn't quite fit into the type of stories they were buying. No further move was made to get it published and it ended up in a box in a family-archival section.

Three decades moved on. Personal elderliness ordered that house accumulations be sorted out and some things discarded. Opening the special box labeled with the book's title, Althea sat and read it—twice. After sharing it with special knowledgeable and helpful friends, the decision was made to tour through the self-publishing route—an enlightening trail.

ACKNOWLEDGEMENTS

Anyone touring through a self-publishing route with enlightened trailblazers can certainly be grateful for every part of the process. When the manuscript for *Secret of the Swans* was recently removed from a secondhand box where it had been hiding for nearly three decades, the first thought was whether we should try to do something with it. When a good friend asked to read it and then offered to type it out for editing and evaluation, the journey was well on its way. With sincere appreciation and gratitude, we've been overwhelmed by the quality of help and guidance for the whole publishing process.

Very special thanks go the following folks who have spent hours manipulating through the qualifying procedures necessary for the final publishing: Kari Rogers, Mary Odden, and graphic artist Kari Odden of Moontide Design who also did the cover and book formats. In the meantime, Mary Howarth-Hernandez took pictures and often rescued the author whose computer savvy needed improvement on a frequent basis. The swan picture on the front cover is from a watercolor painting by our son, Randy Hughes. Special gratitude to my spouse, Kenneth, who offered patience, encouragement, and a willingness to carve out wooden swans. Thankful for enlightened trailblazers? You bet!